Mr. Ricky's Life of Logic.

A taxi-driver's pathway to a better life for all.

Evan Phillips

Introduction

For centuries humans have hurt their fellow-humans for illogical and ridiculous reasons, created by the indoctrination and conditioning they acquired in their childhood and teenage years. Some of these absurd beliefs include racism, misogyny, hating other religions and homophobia. I believe that if these nonsensical beliefs can be eradicated and replaced with more logical ones, we would all treat each other much better.

In this novel, I have tried to portray and present this unintelligent thinking and modes of behavior through the conversations and relationships between a taxi-driver, Mr. Ricky, and the visitors he drives around on the beautiful island of St. Thomas. But the interesting discussions and camaraderie are not enough for him, and he is constantly endeavoring to make them see, with some success, that the rules we all live by can be made better.

Mr. Voltaire said many years ago, that those who can make us believe absurdities can make us commit atrocities, and a lot of atrocities have been committed throughout history. I do believe though that through education and seeing the reality of societal behavior, we can overcome the absurd beliefs we've held on to for so long. Mr. John Lennon sang, "Imagine All the People Living Life in Peace." Wouldn't that be wonderful? Like Mr. Lennon, I too am an optimist.

For my wife, Mary Anne, who has taught me for over half a
century
That true love is not what you say,
But what you do.

Mr. Ricky's Life of Logic.

A taxi-driver's pathway to a better life for all.

Evan Phillips

Table Of Contents

About Author

Evan Phillips: Originally from Guyana, where he grew up during the country's political transformation from British Colonialism to independence, often accompanied by periods of political rhetoric, physical destruction and violence.

He was a junior Tennis champion and attended university in the U.S. on a tennis scholarship. He attained B.A.'s in Eng. Literature and Sociology from Oral Roberts University and an M.A. in Writing and Rhetoric from Tulsa University.

Evan has been a Tennis Pro most of his life in St. Thomas, U.S.Virgin Is. and Tucson, AZ. He has also taught English in High School and at the College level. He has always been an avid student of Human Society.

In this novel, Mr. Ricky, a St. Thomas Taxi-Driver is committed to improving life by trying to convince the tourists he drives to take a closer look at their social conditioning, the illogical rules of society, and improve them through the use of logic.

These rules have led to racism, sexism, homophobia, religionism, etc. and need to be eradicated.

Inspired by John Lennon's great song of hope, Imagine, Phillips has created Mr. Ricky, a refreshingly unique character, in a very interesting story, filled with developing friendships and deep, dark historical facts, with some fascinating surprises as it moves along. If Mr. Ricky and Coach Phillips can get us to pause and examine the rules for life we follow, and change them for the better, perhaps we CAN live more enlightened and peaceful lives.

Chapter One

C hapter One

It was the first week of February, the middle of the tourist season on the island of St. Thomas in the U.S. Virgin Islands. Barry Liburd, six feet tall, slender, with a perpetual smile on his dark, mustachioed face, as if he was constantly saying "what can I do for you today", was the bartender at the Sapphire Beach Bar. It was ten in the morning, and the beach was busy. Many people, most of whom were extremely pale or burnt dangerously red from the tropical sun were casually lying, standing or softly sauntering around on the bright, white sand. Some were in the calm water of Sapphire Bay, soaking in the overwhelming beauty of their vacation circumstances. Many years ago the local tourist board started calling their islands "the American Paradise", and they were right.

The bar was beginning to fill up with most of the patrons drinking bloody marys and screwdrivers at this time of day. A local, dark-skinned, bespectacled man, stocky and wearing a pale blue guayabera shirt and carrying a large bunch of keys, sat down at the far end of the bar. He dropped the keys on the bar, then pulled his chair closer. When Barry heard the keys, he turned and grinned at him.

"Mornin' Ricky, I figure that was you. Workin' the taxi today eh?"

"Mornin' man. Absolutely, a lot of tourists on the island these days. Gotta strike while the iron is hot. Besides the hotel visitors, we have a whole bunch of cruise ships coming in this week."

"That will be great for all of us," Barry said. "What can I get for you?"

"Dark rum an' coke please."

"An' the first one is on me," the bartender said, placing the dark drink in front of the taxi-driver.

"Thank you sir. Appreciate dat. Cheers." He took a big gulp.

"So you driving the taxi van all de time, or you got someone helping you? Because I know you got the government work too."

"I just doin' one or two days a week. I have a partner who does the other days. My son going to be old enough to drive next year, so I'll be able to teach him about business."

"That's a good thing," said Barry. "More kids on this island need to learn about stuff like that. They need to know how the world works, how we make a living' to pay the bills."

Just then an older couple pulled out the bar-chairs and sat down on the opposite side from the two men. Barry heard them, turned quickly, like a ballerina doing a pirouette, and went to serve them. Ricky stretched his arms out, shoulder-high to the

2

side, yawned, then pulled them in and slowly looked around the oblong bar. He had dropped off a group at the Coral World aquarium, and was waiting for them to call and tell him what time they wanted him to pick them up. An overweight gentleman, quite pale, with red hair cut extra short, wearing a yellow t-shirt with a dolphin on it and red shorts that were too big for him, sat down two seats to the left of Ricky.

"Couldn't get the little lady out of bed to save my life this morning," he said, leaning over towards Ricky. "Must be hard to get up early in this paradise. It's beautiful here. Just beautiful." He looked at Ricky, waiting for a response.

Ricky looked at his drink, took a sip, picked up his cell phone, flipped it open and looked at it, took another sip and then turned his head slowly to the left and looked at "yellow shirt".

"Good mornin' sir," he said. "And yes, it is beautiful here."

Just then Ricky's cell phone rang. Once again he picked it up off the bar, flipped it open and spoke with the leader of the Coral World group who asked him to pick them up at eleven. He informed the group leader that there was more to see at Coral World than they realized, and that they should take their time and see as much as they could, and he would come for them at noon, and take them to lunch. The leader agreed, and Ricky hung up. He looked at yellow-shirt again, and saw that he was about to order a drink from Barry.

"Good morning, sir, I trust you're well this fine day. What can I get for you?"

"Man, you people say good morning a lot around here. So good morning," he said with a broad smile."

"Yes, we do. Like to be polite."

"How about an ice-cold screwdriver. That should hit the spot."

"Coming right up," Barry replied and he went to make the drink.

The pale man in the yellow t-shirt turned to Ricky.

"So you're a taxi-driver. Heard you on the phone. So is business pretty good?" he asked with a slight twang, so that "pretty" sounded like a foreign word.

"Yes, it's busy right now, but it's seasonal like many businesses on a vacation island. Most of our visitors are from the U.S. mainland, so they come here in the winter months to get away from the cold weather. They're having a snow storm in the northeast today. I think the high temp in Boston today is nineteen, so that means ice too."

"That's real cold. I'm from Tulsa, Oklahoma, and it's not as cold there as the northeast, but we can have some pretty cold days at this time of year too."

"Don't come across too many people from Oklahoma here in the V.I. You like it there?"

"Been there my whole life. It's a nice place. Good people there. Down to earth, solid. You know ah, conservative."

"No, I don't know. So what brought you to St. Thomas?"

"The wife's brother. He lives in New Jersey and has been here four or five times; so he tells us the next time we go to the

Caribbean, we should go to St. Thomas because the people are really nice there, the place is beautiful and it's also part of the U.S. We went to Puerto Rico two years ago, but didn't like it much. And they're part of the U.S. too."

"Trouble with the Spanish?" Ricky asked.

"No, not really. You can get used to that. It was like they didn't want us there."

"Well, we certainly want you here. Welcome to the U.S. Virgin Islands."

"I'll drink to that. Cheers." And he took a swig of his drink and raised his glass. "Ah, that's good," he exclaimed. "By the way, name's Earl, Earl Francis." He reached over and thrust his right hand towards Ricky, who took it weakly and gently shook.

"Ricky, Ricky Brin."

"So Ricky, I was reading the local papers this morning before leaving my room and I see your senators were debating some bill for a tax increase. Something about needing more funding for schools and roads. For a moment I thought I was back in Tulsa again. You know, we're getting a certain liberal element there, especially around the university and some areas of the city, where they believe that paying more taxes will solve all our problems."

"I guess how much citizens pay in taxes is discussed in many places. And also what kind of taxes. For example, in the Bahamas they don't have income taxes, but you have to pay fairly high duties on some products not made or grown in the Caribbean."

"But as a businessman, you don't believe in paying high taxes to the government? Do you?"

"I guess it depends on what you consider high."

"Well personally, I would welcome a world that didn't pay no taxes. I get tired of paying a bunch of my profits to the damn government."

"So what about schools and roads," Ricky said with a smile, "who would pay for those?"

Earl looked at him with his mouth opening, as though he wanted to say something, but he didn't, waiting for Ricky to finish.

"Now don't get me wrong," Ricky said, "I don't enjoy paying some of the taxes I pay, but I think it is a responsibility we all have to share in order for society to work better."

He took the last sip of his drink, looked at the empty glass momentarily, then raised it in the air, telling Barry that he wanted another one. The bartender mixed the beverage, then came over to Ricky and placed it in front of him. The two men smiled at each other, then Barry took the empty glass away.

"And this one's on me," Earl said loudly. The bartender waved his arm to acknowledge his offer. Ricky bowed his head gently and said thanks.

"So what do you do in Tulsa?" Ricky asked.

"I'm in the oil business. I work for a small family owned company that was started in the nineteen twenties."

"So you been in Tulsa your whole life?"

6

"Pretty much. Went to college there. University of Tulsa. Got married there. Three kids. And still living there."

"And paid a lot of taxes there over the years." Ricky said smiling.

"Yeah. A lotta taxes. I'm not sure it's even a part of our constitution, but it sure makes our gov'ment stronger. I believe people should make their own decisions and not be told what to do all the time. After all, it's supposed to be a free country. Right?"

"Well, I don't think freedom means you don't pay taxes. And I don't think the founding fathers said all men are free. They said all of us are created equal."

"You guys are a U.S. territory. Right?"

Ricky nodded.

"And you study the U.S. constitution and history and all that gov'ment stuff."

"We sure do," Ricky said. He really didn't want to get into a long drawn out conversation about American history with this tourist, but by the same token he was going to say what he thought and not just agree with him.

"So, do you know what the Boston Tea Party was?"

"Sure. I remember the tea party."

"Well, that was all about not paying taxes," Earl said emphatically. "The early Americans didn't want to pay taxes. So they had riots and eventually fought against the British and formed their own sovereign country. They didn't believe they should pay taxes."

Ricky looked across at Barry, who was obviously hearing the conversation the two men were having, smiled, and shook his head. Ricky shrugged his shoulders and then leaned over a little closer to Earl.

"As far as I can remember from my government classes," he said in a quieter voice, "the Tea Party wasn't just about taxation or not payin' taxes, it was about taxation without representation."

"What do you mean?"

"It means that they were a colony and were told to pay taxes. They couldn't vote for the people who told them to pay the taxes, so they didn't have representation. The King of England could tell them to pay anything in taxes, and if they didn't, they would be arrested."

"You sure about that?"

"Yes I am." He nodded his head boldly and smiled.

"You know I have some friends back in Oklahoma who believe that the constitution doesn't say anything about paying taxes, especially income taxes, and so it's illegal. Now I'm not a constitutional scholar, but I tend to agree with them."

"Well you can't really agree with someone unless you understand what they're talking about. You can't just say you agree with them because you'll make more money. That's not logical. The Supreme Court did rule that paying taxes was constitutional. It was in the early nineteen hundreds. I believe it was the ah, ah, sixteenth amendment."

"You know for a taxi-driver on a tourist island, you know a lot about our constitution."

"We have a pretty good public school system in the V.I. And, maybe we also want to prove that we're good Americans, so we pay close attention to things like history and government. And of course the taxpayer makes sure that we have good public schools," he added with a wry smile.

"There you go again, the taxpayer paying for stuff that not everybody uses. My kids go to private school and I pay for them. Why should I pay for public school too? Somehow that seems to take away some of my freedom. Don't you think, ah, Ricky? I mean don't we have the freedom to choose where we want to send our children to school? In our case we're pretty religious and we want to send them to a school that teaches them about the Lord, and I don't think they do that much in public school anymore."

Ricky took a deep breath and let it out slowly, then another sip of his rum and coke. He looked at Earl and smiled. "Earl, my friend, I don't know if you really want to get into this stuff w'en you here relaxing on vacation. Maybe we should just let it go."

"No, no, not at all. We just having a friendly chat at a bar. I'd like to hear what you have to say. Your culture is a little different than mine, and I'd really like to hear what you think. If you don't mind."

"Ok, well here is what I think. I think you have to be careful with the word 'freedom'. It doesn't mean that you can do whatever you want, because if everyone does whatever they want we would have chaos. So we have to have some rules to follow, and these rules are called laws. Another word is regulations."

"But don't you think we have too many damn laws?"

"Maybe, but what if we had no laws at all?"

"I didn't say we should get rid of every law."

"But who's to say that we have too many or too few. You have to take everyone into consideration, not just those who agree with you."

"So what is freedom to you?"

"Well the constitution gives us the right or the freedom to criticize any law we don't agree with. We can do that on t.v. or in the newspapers or any other outlet. We also have the freedom to march and protest peacefully against any law. But if we do it violently or cause property damage or hurt people, then we can be arrested and charged. And of course, at the next election we can vote for representatives who will make a different law or get rid of the one we don't like."

"So once you have a law you have to obey it, even if you totally disagree with it?"

"Well, if you choose not to obey it and you're caught, you can be arrested and prosecuted."

"You sure you're not a teacher or a lawyer or something official?"

"I'm not any of those. Just a taxi-driver. I do some other things, like many people, to help pay the bills, but at heart, I'm just a taxi-driver, and even though I would like to send my children to private schools, I can't afford it. So the only way they can get a high school education is to send them to public schools, and the only way there can be public schools is for the tax-payer to pay for them. And the public schools have to be pretty good, or else the kids who go to the private schools would always be ahead of them, and they would always be in second place."

"But wouldn't it be great if we all had a choice and we could send our kids to private school if we wanted to?"

"That would be nice, but who's going to pay for the private school?" Ricky's shoulders started to shake and he laughed softly. "Mr. Earl, are you suggesting that we all pay more taxes to send all the kids in the U.S. to private school. My God, there are more than a hundred million children."

Earl looked at him, shook his head slowly and then smiled broadly. "You have a point my friend. I guess we have to think this through more carefully. But I still believe that there's a better way to educate our kids than what we have right now."

"I certainly agree with that," said Ricky. "And now I have to get back to work. Hope I run into you again. I'm often here in the evenings after work." He pushed his chair back, gently shook Earl's hand, left a tip for Barry under his glass, told him to put his bill on his tab, then turned and slowly walked away from the bar and the beach, and out into the parking lot.

Chapter Two

C hapter Two

It was Sunday late afternoon at the Sapphire Beach Bar, and there was the sweet sound of steel-band music in the air as the sun was going down in the cloudy, western sky. The bar was full with both guests and locals, as the Sapphire Beach Sunday party was a popular island event. Barry was extremely busy pouring drinks and making sure that none of his customers waited very long when they needed a libation. He was assisted on Sundays by his nephew Clifford, who also tended bar on the island. The two were an efficient operation. At this time there were still some people on the beach who came up to the bar for drinks, and these were Cliff's priority. He made sure they were served in a timely fashion, and also used plastic cups, as glass was not allowed on the beach.

The steel-band was playing some of the old, slow, Caribbean classics: "Yellow Bird" and "Jamaica Farewell" among them. If one listened carefully, one could almost hear Harry Belafonte's voice, crooning the words, "daylight come an' me want go home", with the gentle waves of the Caribbean Sea in the background, washing up on the beach.

There was a dance-floor in front of the steel-band, next to the bar, and a few couples were dancing. They were all talking and laughing as they held each other and moved in time to the music, as if they'd just met.

And Earl Francis was there. He was wearing a bright, yellow, Hawaiian shirt, and looked as though he really was related to the yellow bird in the banana tree. He had a bottle of Corona beer in front of him and was smiling and swaying to the steel-band music. In contrast to the yellow shirt was his body complexion. It was bright red, dangerously red. He had obviously spent too much time in the sun without adequate sunscreen protection. He saw Barry serving the customer two seats to his right, and waved vigorously to get his attention.

"Hey Barry, my man. Over here."

"Hello, Mr. Francis. How you doin'? Sorry I can't talk now, real busy. How can I help you?"

"This is a great party, my man, how about a dark rum and coke. Enough beer for one day."

"Coming right up. Yeah, Sunday evenings are good fun. Always a nice crowd."

"And also good business," Earl yelled.

"Here you go. Let me know when you need another." Barry was gone, already serving his next customer.

The tempo of the music was faster now, as the band had sped up the tempo. Earl started moving faster as well, side to side, then forward and back in time to the calypso beat. His eyes were closed and he appeared to be under some magical spell. He felt a firm tap on his right shoulder and heard a familiar voice.

"You goin' to wear yourself out if you keep up this pace."

It was Ricky.

Earl jumped to his feet, turned quickly, and put one hand on his friend's shoulder as he clumsily shook his hand.

"How you been, my man? Busy? Isn't this band great?"

"I've been well. Yes I've been busy, and this is an excellent band. I see you've spent a lot of time in our sun."

"Yes, fell asleep for two hours with no shade yesterday. Didn't mean to. I know how important it is to go slowly when it comes to lying in the sun. Just fell asleep out in the open. No shade."

"Have you put anything on it? Any aloe? If you're not careful that could turn into a burn, and they are really painful."

"Well I've been putting on sunscreen since I woke up, an' I've been trying to stay under the umbrella too."

"I tell you what, I believe the beach store is still open. I'll go get some aloe for you and be back soon. I don't like how red your skin is."

Ten minutes later he returned with a refrigerated bottle of aloe gel.

"Here, got you some aloe, go in the bathroom and put it on your exposed skin, and don't rub it in too much."

Earl returned to the bar engulfed in a heavy coat of aloe gel. Ricky chuckled and then smiled at him.

"That should do the trick," he said.

"How do I look?"

"Like you fell into a barrel of glue," he said, laughing harder this time.

"You always this honest?" Earl asked.

"Yes he is," Barry said to the visitor as he walked by, inside the bar, with two glasses in his hands.

"There's a couple of seats at a table in the back," Ricky said. "Let's go sit over there so we can hear ourselves talk a little better."

Earl, red as a lobster just pulled out of the ocean, followed him to the empty table. Before the men could sit down, a smiling, light-brown complexioned young woman, with a pink hibiscus flower in her hair, took their drink order.

"Good afternoon, Mister Ricky," she said with a slight bow to Ricky, "what can I get for you?"

"Two dark Cruzan and cokes would be good, thanks."

"A lot of people on the island seem to know you."

"Small island. So where's your wife? Thought she might enjoy the music and some dancing."

"She had a long day on the beach and went to take a nap."

"Hope she didn't get as much sun as you."

"No, she's not as dumb as me. She made sure she was in the shade most of the time."

"That's good, one sunburn patient is enough. Actually, I think we caught it in time. Another exposed day in the sun and you would have been in a lot of pain."

"Well, I'm most grateful. By the way, what do I owe you for the aloe?" he asked, fumbling for his wallet in his back pocket.

"Not a thing. For a little emergency matter such as this, the island is more than happy to be of service to our guests and friends."

"Then you must let me take care of your drinks. The least I can do."

"That I would not stop you from doing."

The waitress returned with their drinks, placed them on the table in front of the two men and quickly hurried off. Ricky picked his up.

"Cheers, my friend," he said, then took a sip of the cold rum and coke.

The two men drank in silence and looked at the dance-floor. Earl seemed quite fascinated by the couples dancing. There were white couples, black couples, and quite a few whites dancing with blacks. There was also a group of three Indian girls who were dancing with both blacks and whites.

"You know that's a strange sight even for me, and I consider myself to be quite hip."

"What's that?"

"You know, ah the different races dancing with each other."

"Why is that?"

"Well, you know, back in the States the different races tend to keep to their own race."

"And why is that?"

"It's just the way it is. I guess they just feel more comfortable with people who look and sound like them. And then there are some people who feel it's wrong for the races to mix. They even say it's biblical."

"So do these people just say it's biblical or do they actually point it out to you? I'm a very good student of the Bible, and I don't know of any place where it says that."

"Now I'm not saying it's good or bad. I personally don't have anything against anyone who's a different race. I'm just telling you how it is."

"So you believe it's in the Bible?"

"Well, you know when your Pastor says something to you, you can't exactly ask him if it's in the Bible. You have to believe he knows what's in it; that's why he's the Pastor."

"So he can tell you anything and say it's in the Bible? and you being a Christian would believe him."

"Yes, that's pretty much how it works. To be honest I never thought about it that much."

"But you went to college. Don't you believe in logic? In asking questions?"

"Religion is not about logic or questions. I believe it's about faith." Earl's voice was louder now, and he quickly drained his rum and coke and signaled the waitress to bring two more.

Ricky smiled to himself and looked at his half-empty glass, debating internally whether to change the topic or continue along the same line. He decided to continue.

"I hope I'm not making you feel uncomfortable, but aren't you a little concerned that someone could completely control your life and make you believe anything they want you to, good or bad? All they have to do is tell you what to believe, based on illogical myths, hearsay and assumptions and throw in the word, faith."

The waitress brought the drinks. Earl took a sip of his, laughed and turned his head to look at Ricky.

"How come when we start having a friendly conversation, you start to sound more like a philosopher or a professor than a taxi-driver?"

"Well my friend, over the years I've driven a lot of different people around, and as you now know I probably talk too much and ask too many questions, so I learn a lot of things. Driving a taxi can give you a good education."

"I never thought of the taxi business that way, but you make a good point."

"So let's say that what your pastor said about segregation in the Bible is not true. Why do you think it's strange to see people of different races dancing?"

"I'm not really sure. I guess I'm just not used to it, so it makes me uncomfortable. I don't believe I ever went to a dance back home where African Americans and Whites danced together."

"You mean African Americans and European Americans."

"I don't follow you."

"You can say blacks and whites, but if you say African American then logically you have to say European American."

"Never thought about it that way, but I guess if you're speaking proper English, you're right."

"So do you think people of different races should mix at all?"

"Of course they should mix, I didn't say anything about not mixing."

"So it's okay for them to talk to each other?"

"Of course," Earl said with a sheepish smile. "Of course they can talk."

"So they can talk and mix, but they shouldn't dance with each other? Is that your basic position or feeling?"

"I'm beginning to feel as though I'm being cross-examined in court."

"No, not at all, my friend. We're just having a friendly chat about the different way of life between the Mainland and the Islands. No worries." Ricky laughed and patted Earl on the shoulder.

The two men drank in silence for a while, listening to the band play some faster calypso music. Earl was staring at the dancers, especially the local females, who were gyrating their hips in perfect time with the calypso beat. The music stopped, and the band leader announced he would be taking a fifteen minute break.

"That was great," Earl proclaimed, "and those ladies can really dance. They look like professionals."

"Yes, we learn to dance to calypso music early in this part of the world. Some people say the rhythm is in our DNA, but I just think it's something we've learned and become used to and now it's part of our culture."

"So if I lived here, I would be able to dance the calypso like that?"

"Of course, I would teach you myself," Ricky said with a loud chuckle.

"So even though I'm white."

"Of course, that's got nothing to do with it. White Virgin Islanders can all dance calypso. They learn the beat from childhood, just like local children of any other race."

"So if a child was say, Chinese, and they were born here, they would learn to move and dance like the black children?"

"As long as they were taught the moves by whoever raised them, or even by their friends."

"That's another interesting point," Earl said shaking his head and laughing. "You have so many of them. You must really talk to a lot of people when you drive that taxi."

"Yes I do. I also happen to believe that to some extent we're all products of what we were taught and conditioned to believe, when we were very young."

"That's why it's so important for parents to do their job and raise their kids properly."

"What if the parents don't know what properly is? What if they don't have parents, or know them?"

"There you go again, you're always asking these tough questions."

"Yes you're right," Ricky said. "We need to relax and enjoy the music and our drinks."

The band started playing again, and the men sat in silence, sipping their drinks. Earl moved his head from side to side, and appeared quite strange looking with his lobster complexion and very white teeth. There was a couple dancing in the middle of the floor, and Earl looked closely at them. The young woman was wearing a bright-green bikini top with a very short pair of denim shorts, and was being twirled around by her partner. Both dancers had dark tans, but she appeared to be white and her partner, black.

"Now, that one over there," Earl said pointing to the young lady in the bikini top out to Ricky, with his bright-red chin. "That one there in the bikini, looks like she could have benefited from better parenting when she was younger."

"So look who's bringing up the serious topic now." He looked at the girl then looked back at Earl. "So, what's bothering you about her?"

"Well, the way she's dancing is so suggestive. She's moving her hips from side to side and then round and round, like she's trying to seduce him or something. Then they're dancing cheek to cheek with arms wrapped around each other. Back home we would say that she needs some good religion. If she had that she wouldn't behave this way."

Ricky let his head drop, chin touching his chest, and looked at the table for a couple of minutes. Then he looked at Earl and slowly shook his head.

"What, you don't agree with me? You don't think if she had some good, strong religious training she would behave more ah, morally and ah, lady-like?"

"First things first. Let's have another drink and also get something to eat. Maybe some French fries." He waved to the waitress, motioned for her to come over, and gave her the order.

"Earl, how do you know that young lady doesn't go to church on a regular basis?"

"I don't think she would behave like that if she went to church. She would be more mindful of not appearing so sexual, especially in a public place."

"But different places have different cultures. People dance differently in this part of the world than they do in Oklahoma, or Nebraska or say, Kansas. You're not used to seeing Caribbean women dance, so you assume it's immoral. You are prejudging them without any facts, just assumptions. That's what prejudice is."

"I thought prejudice had to do with race."

"It does have to do with race, but that's only one form of prejudice. There are many others. Prejudice against Women, against Gay people, people from different parts of a country, farmers, city-people and on and on."

"You're right, I never thought of that."

"Earl I know you were fortunate enough to go to a fine university, and you did the hard work to graduate, but did you ever do a class in basic sociology?"

"I've never really been interested in that social stuff. There were a couple of classes I really didn't pay much attention to. I think that kind of thinking just causes problems and it's better to avoid them. Besides, with all the competition in the world of business, you have to put all your attention and effort on business to do well. To study about sociology or even psychology, would be to take away from that. And it was always important for me to do well in my college major, get a good job, and have a family that I could support and provide for."

"So you saw your college education as mainly a place to develop a job skill?"

"What else is it? I mean you have a little fun along the way, but basically you go there to get good job skills so you can get a good job. Otherwise, why go?"

"So in a way you're saying that besides getting a good job skill, you already knew most of what you needed to deal with life. You didn't feel you needed to learn more about history, or psychology or geography, maybe some political science?"

Earl looked at the young lady in the bathing suit top and smiled, shaking his head.

"I guess you could say I already knew most of those things from high school. And I was comfortable with how I lived. I was taught right from wrong by my folks, especially my Dad, and had a good religious upbringing and went to church regularly. And I think that when I was growing up I was kind to people, but also tough, so people wouldn't take advantage of me. My Dad was big on that."

"So when you said that young lady in the bathing suit top needed religion. What religion were you talking about?"

"Well I only know one religion, and that's the Christian religion. And I don't mean the Catholics or the Church of England. I mean the Evangelical Christians, where they pray and speak to God in plain English, and not in Latin or some other foreign language."

"Did you ever think of what other religions are like?"

"You mean like the Jews?"

"No, I mean like the Muslims, or maybe the Hindus?"

"No, I started a class in comparative religions, but thought it was boring, so I dropped it. I mean if I believe my religion is the one true religion, then what do I need to study others for? I could end up confusing myself."

"That's a good point," Ricky said and laughed. "The last thing you want to do relating to religion, is make it confusing. It should be very simple as it was intended to be."

"Amen. Keep it simple. That's what I believe. And I think that's what the good Lord intended. Simple."

"So you believe that if everyone kept religion simple the world would be a better place?"

"Yes I do."

"And you're talking about the Christian religion?"

"Yes I am. Only one I know."

"Does it matter which denomination?"

"Not really, Baptist, Pentecostal, even the Methodists. All pretty much the same. Praising God and following the Lord."

"What about Catholics?"

"No they're different. I don't view them as Christian, it's like they have their own separate religion: with the Virgin Mary and the confessions and the way they put their hand in Holy Water to make the sign of the cross. They're just different."

"Do you believe in the Virgin Mary?"

Earl stopped talking and sat still for a few minutes. He took a sip from his drink, looked at the dance-floor, and then turned to look at Ricky.

"You know, this conversation is getting a little deep."

"I believe if you look closely enough at anything that humans do, you'll find it's pretty deep."

"So, do you know much about the Catholics, my friend?"

"Well, I actually went to a Catholic high school, even though I, myself wasn't Catholic. So, you could say I know a fair amount about them."

"And don't you think their religion is strange?"

"Most Catholics I know would say the same thing about what you believe."

"Really!"

"Yes. Also, Catholicism is not a religion, it's a denomination of Christianity. For about twelve or thirteen hundred years it was the only Christian denomination. Catholics were the only Christians."

"I'll take your word for that. So when did it change? When did the Protestants come into the picture?"

"Let's have another drink, and relax a bit. This conversation is starting to get heavy, and I don't want you to feel like I'm imposing on you."

"No, no, not at all. You're not imposing. This all sounds interesting coming from you. Keep going. I believe we should also have a drink, but keep going."

Ricky ordered the drinks, and then returned to the conversation.

"Okay, so the Christian church, which was of course led by the Pope, started having some very controversial policies, and one of them was selling indulgences, or pardons. So if you had an enemy, you could burn down his house, which is a terrible sin, but if you paid a certain amount of money to the Church, the Pope would grant you a pardon, and the act of burning down the house would not be a sin."

The waitress brought the drinks, set them down on the table, smiled sweetly at Ricky, and then left.

"Please continue."

"Well, there were a few academically inclined monks, and they thought that this was a terrible idea, so they protested against the Pope's policy. The most prominent of these monks, was the German, Martin Luther, and he was a protester, a Protestant."

"You know, I seem to remember something about that from a world history class in college that I obviously didn't pay enough attention to. And the name Luther is also coming back to me. And when was this?"

"Around the first half of the sixteenth century. But more stuff happened around that same time." Ricky paused and took a sip of his drink.

"Go on. What else happened?"

"You sure you want to hear more about this stuff now? It gets a little heavy; if you know what I mean," he said with a wink.

"Yes, yes, I want to hear it. Now you have me on the edge of my seat," he said laughing.

" Ok: well, you know who Henry the Eighth was?"

"Yes, the king who had a whole bunch of wives."

"Good, good. Well right around the same time as Luther's actions, Henry, who was King of England, decided he wanted to divorce his wife, Katherine. Now remember all the Christian countries at this time were still Catholic, and the Catholic Church didn't allow divorce. So the Pope told Henry that he could have all the women he wanted, but he couldn't divorce Katherine. So Henry told the Pope that he was a great King, and no Pope could tell him what to do, so he divorced Katherine, married another woman, and formed his own English religion, called the Anglican Church. He protested against the rules of the Catholic Church, so the Anglicans were also Protestants. And of course the name of the church that Luther formed, was called....?"

"Lutherans," Earl said slowly.

"Exactly. This is just basic history, telling how Protestantism came about. Where the problem comes in, is when people believe that their religion, or even their denomination is better than what someone else believes, to the point of actually hurting them, or worse."

"For example?"

"How about the Catholics and Anglicans in Ireland?"

"Yes, now that you mention it, I remember that. And I believe the British Government was involved too."

"Yes, two groups basically killing each other over religion, even though the religion is practically identical."

"So you're saying Catholics and Protestants believe in the same things?"

"Yes, they do. There may be a few small differences, but the fundamentals are the same."

"And you learned all this stuff in high school?"

"Most of it. Some I studied on my own. And I also went to the local college we have here for a while. Of course I had that advantage of not being Catholic in a Catholic school. I was brought up a Methodist, so being a curious person I wanted to find out what made them so different from me, and I came to the realization that they really weren't. I was also a Sunday School teacher for a while, so I had to know the doctrine I was teaching."

"So you're telling me that I should have studied the various Christian religions, ah, I mean denominations when I was in college?"

"Well, it wouldn't have been a bad idea to figure out what you really believed in, instead of accepting what someone told you."

"Yes, but my parents taught me religion, and they were Evangelicals. They believed I should be religious and this was the best one, which they learned from their parents. And I believe it's best for my kids."

Ricky sensed his friend getting somewhat defensive.

"I apologize. I didn't want this to sound as though I'm against your religion, but the point I'm trying to make is that humans can be very rational, logical beings. When you were deciding what business to go into after college, I'm sure you didn't just jump into the first one that came along. You probably studied several of them and carefully picked the one that you thought suited you, and would also be profitable. But we tend to believe everything our parents, or the people who raised us, told us. It's called conditioning. But this also leads to beliefs about race, or how men treat women, or how we feel about animals or what kinds of foods we eat. And unless some event changes how we feel, maybe something like going to college, we're condemned to believe what we were taught for our entire lifetimes."

"Have you always felt like this?"

"Not at all. In fact I felt very much the way you did for a long time, just more or less believing what I was taught by my parents. Pretty much like you. What I believe now, is just life being something real, logical, without being influenced by supernatural or made-up events. And trying to make it better through kindness and caring for others."

"How old are you, Rick, if you don't mind my asking?"

"I turned fifty, three months ago."

"Wow, I must say you seem a lot younger than that. I would have guessed late thirties."

"Well thank you my friend," Rick said with a laugh. "Must be the light in here and the alcohol. They both have a way of making things look better than they are."

"I'll drink to that."

The band took another break and Ricky looked at his watch. It was getting late and time for him to go home. He had a full day tomorrow. But there was one more thing he wanted his friend Earl to do before he left. He wanted him to meet and have a few words with the young lady who had disturbed him so much on the dance floor. He pushed his chair back and stood up, told Earl that he would be right back, and walked through the Sunday night crowd to the other side of the bar where she was.

"Good evening, Miss Danette," he said with a small bow. "I trust you're enjoying yourself."

"Hi, Mr. Rick, I thought that was you sitting over there. Yes, I'm enjoying myself. I haven't seen you out on the dance floor yet."

"No, I've been speaking with a new friend, a visitor. Interesting gentleman. Would you mind coming over for a few minutes and meeting him?"

"Not at all. Just let me tell my boyfriend and I'll be right there."

Ricky walked back to the table, pulled out his chair with a squeak, and sat opposite Earl.

"I saw you talking to that girl; the one in the bikini. You know her?"

"As a matter of fact I do. She's going to join us shortly."

"No way. Really?"

"Yes. Really."

Before Earl could say anything else, Lorraine Danette was standing in front of them.

Both men jumped to their feet, and Ricky introduced Earl to Lorraine. She looked different than when she had been dancing. Her hair was pulled back in a ponytail, and she was wearing a large, light blue t-shirt, with the letters V. I. on it, over her bikini-top.

"It's very nice to meet you, Lorraine. I was just telling my new friend, Ricky, what a good dancer you are. I have to try to learn the ah, ah, rhythm of this island music so that I can enjoy it as well. It is quite different from the type of music I'm used to back in Oklahoma."

"Can we get you something to drink?" Ricky asked. "You must be thirsty after all that dancing."

"Yes, thanks. A coke would be nice."

Ricky motioned to the waitress, ordered the coke, and then sat down.

"So, I guess your Spring holidays are coming to an end, and you're back in school later this week."

"Yes, we go back on Thursday. One more semester and then graduation."

"So that's why you're dancing and partying, you're on vacation, like me," Earl said, trying to get into the conversation. "And you're going to graduate in a few months. Well congratulations!"

"Thank you, sir. Seems like I've been in high school a long time."

The waitress came with Lorraine's coke and she took a couple of big sips.

"So, what do you do next, after high school, I mean? Are you going to stay on the island? You guys have a community college or something like that here, don't you? Maybe you're going to go there?"

"Actually, the University of the Virgin Islands is a four year school, but Lorraine is going to college in your neck of the woods."

"And where would that be?"

This time Lorraine answered. "At the University of Texas, in Austin."

"U of T, wow. That's a great school. And what do you plan to study there?"

"I'll probably do my bachelor's in political science, and then go to law school there as well."

"Well congratulations, young lady. It's nice to hear someone your age sound so sure and positive about their future."

"Not only that," Ricky said. "She has a full academic scholarship."

"That's great. Can I at least buy you another coke?"

"Sure," she said, finishing the drink in front of her.

"So, I take it you guys know each other," Earl said, gesturing towards Ricky with a nod of his head. "Seems like everyone knows my good friend. At least around here."

"It's a small island, and Mr. Ricky does a lot of things in our community, and has a lot of friends, so a lot of people know him."

"So how do you know him?"

"Well, he's pretty good friends with my parents, and he also used to teach Sunday School in my church when I was quite young."

"I hope you don't think I'm too nosy, but I'm trying to get a feel for the island. The people are really very interesting. So what do your parents do?"

"They own a small hardware store, but my mother is also an accountant, mostly taxes."

"And did they both go to college?"

"Yes, they did."

"Let me guess. Texas?"

"Only my mom, my dad went to the University of California at Berkeley."

"That's really good to hear. So important for people to have a college education. That's so different than the ridiculous idea that so many tourists have, myself included, that the people who live on a tourist island just go around selling t-shirts and hats to the visitors, or renting them lounge chairs on the beach, or taking them diving."

"Well some of us actually do those things," Ricky said. "In my case I drive them around on tours to see the island."

"Yes, but you do so much more."

"Maybe," Ricky said with a smile.

"But you know what I mean. A lot of people who live here are also lawyers, and nurses, physicians, bankers, accountants, business people, teachers."

"You mean like regular people," Ricky said with a laugh. "Yes, I guess some of us are regular."

Earl suddenly sat up straight and leaned over the edge of the table, slightly towards Lorraine.

"Before we say anything else," he said. "I have to apologize to Lorraine."

She looked at him quizzically.

"Young lady, earlier tonight when I first saw you dancing, I criticized the way you were dressed, in just your bathing suit top. I told my friend here that I thought it was too ah, ah, risqué for you to be dressed like that in public. Then I realized that others were doing the same, and it must be part of the culture here. So I wish to say I'm sorry."

"Oh," Lorraine said, obviously surprised at the apology. "That's very gracious of you. Thank you. Yes, I imagine the way we dress at a party on the beach, next to the Caribbean Sea, would be somewhat different than the way people would dress at a party in a city in Oklahoma."

"You'd probably be fine in cowboy boots," Ricky said, trying to lighten the mood.

"You're probably right," Earl said. "Hadn't thought of that. You probably prejudge us in Oklahoma as a bunch of ignorant Okies who run around the place with little education and wearing cowboy boots; just like I prejudge you here in the islands as hanging out at the beach all day and selling trinkets to tourists."

"Now you understand how prejudging works. It doesn't take much. But with me it's different, because I know some individuals personally who were educated in Oklahoma, and they're very intelligent people. In fact I have a good friend on St.Thomas who has a Master's in English from the University of Tulsa, and he understands about writing and literature, especially social literature, better than anyone I've ever met. He's actually a tennis coach, and our best player. So if you got the education in your field, that he got in his, I'd say you're very intelligent, whether you wear cowboy boots or not."

Just then a few notes on the rhythm guitar could be heard as the band started warming up for its final session.

"I think that's your cue," Ricky said. "Go and find that handsome boyfriend of yours and enjoy your dancing. Thanks for chatting with us, and don't forget to think about coming to see what that new church is all about."

"It's always good to talk to you Mr. Ricky. I have been thinking about that church, Universal Unitarian, sounds interesting. And nice to meet you Mr. Earl. Enjoy the rest of the evening and enjoy your vacation." Lorraine got up and left.

"That was very gracious of you to apologize to Lorraine," Ricky said, "it kinda surprised me; especially since she never actually heard what you said."

"Well, I been thinking about what you said about prejudging and all that. And here I am being a royal a-hole, prejudging the way someone dresses and maybe even dances and I don't know anything about their culture. Talk about the Ugly American."

"Now, wait a minute, remember we Virgin Islanders are Americans too."

"See, there I go screwing up again. Should have remembered that."

"Well actually that's understandable. It is a different way of life, but more of a sub-culture. Just like the way of life in New York City might seem completely different than the one in Tulsa."

"Yes, professor, let's have one more drink, then I have to turn in. I'm surprised the wife hasn't called me. She's probably asleep." He drained his glass and signaled to the waitress to bring two more drinks.

"So what was that church Lorraine said you were trying to get her to join?" Earl asked as the band started playing again and couples moved on to the dance-floor.

"Oh, it's the U.U. Church. Universalist Unitarian."

Earl rubbed his jaw in thought for a few moments. He smiled broadly, as though quite pleased with himself for remembering something really important.

"You mean like the old Unitarian Church that some of the founding fathers belonged to?"

"Well, yes, I believe it did originally come from the old Unitarian Church, but it's changed a lot, and become more universal, meaning that people can meet there and have very different beliefs."

"Yeah. I've heard it's become pretty radical. Like anyone can go there."

"And you have a problem with just anyone going to a church. I always thought they were all open to everyone."

"Well, what I mean is why would people go to a church if they didn't all believe the same thing?"

"Maybe they're all searching for a greater truth than the simplistic one that's often conveniently packaged and handed to them in traditional churches."

"You said you were a Methodist. Do you think they gave you a prepackaged belief, as you put it? Don't you think you could form your own philosophy?"

"As a matter of fact, when I was old enough to think for myself, I did think their religious teaching was very trite, and made up to make it convenient to condition their members to have a specific belief."

"And you think this Universalist Unitarian Church is different?"

"Very much so. I personally don't believe in the doctrine of any religion that I've come into contact with. They're all completely illogical and made up. But I like the idea of citizens in a community coming together and helping each other, or others in need, and showing an appreciation for the world in which we live. Maybe there's a better meeting place or church out there that would satisfy these desires, but this particular church is the best one that I've found so far."

"So, you don't believe in faith? I always thought that was the foundation of any religion."

"I do have faith, but it is based on logic and reason, not just on say so. I believe that blind faith is a very dangerous position, and has been the cause of much suffering in the world, going back a long, long time."

"So here we are talking about religion again," Earl said with a laugh, "but I must say you make it sound interesting."

"It is interesting, whether you believe in one religion or not. The concept of religion is very interesting. It has been very closely connected with humans for thousands of years. We look at the world around us, and we wonder who created it, if in fact it was created. We know that we have good things happen to us and also bad, and we wonder if some Deity has a say in this. And above all, we all know we're going to die one day, and we want to know what happens to us."

"Never thought about it like that, but I must say I don't really find anything wrong with what you're saying."

"Well, there's not much to be wrong. This is all very general and pretty much factual. What's odd, is that we're taught about religion in a very simplistic, matter of fact manner, that really makes no logical sense; so we call it faith, and over the centuries we've been ready to kill other people because they were taught something different from us in the same illogical manner."

"So, this Unitarian Church, or Universal Unitarian. Do they believe in God?"

"I would say most do, but you don't have to, or you can call God by another name, the Great Spirit, or the Creator for example. But those of us who believe in God, don't believe in the Trinity - the Father, Son and Holy Ghost. We don't believe that Jesus is God, just a great Jewish prophet who preached about the better nature of mankind."

"So what kind of religion is it?"

"Some say it's not a religion at all, just a gathering of friends or citizens if you prefer, who meet and discuss their ideas about spirituality and a search for the truth about life in general, and hopefully try to make it better."

"You know, I live in a pretty conservative, religious town, and I've lived there all my life, but I must say, I've never heard anyone discuss religion the way you do."

"That's because they probably just accept what they've been taught and don't question it. That's my whole point in our little discussion tonight. People feel incredibly strong about the religion they've been taught, but they never examine it. To tell you the truth, Earl, I really don't care what religion anyone believes in, but they should at least understand what they believe in. Religion encompasses some big concepts, astronomical - life, death, creation, human behavior, etc. etc. People should at least take a little time to have a good understanding of what they believe in."

"Can't say I don't agree with that. It's too easy to just go through the motions without doing some thinking."

"Amen to that. Now enough religion for one night."

"Amen to that too."

The two men were silent for a while, looking at each other, smiling, watching the dancers and nodding to the music.

"So, are you working tonight?" Earl asked.

"Had a couple of trips earlier, but they're staying here, so it doesn't look like anything else tonight. Tomorrow I have a trip planned to St. John. If you and your wife don't have anything planned, I'd be happy to take you. It's a full day, very enjoyable. I drive my van to the ferry dock then take the ferry over, then once we get there I use a friend's van to take you around the island. Besides the usual beach activity and some good local food and drinks, I also take you to the ruins of an old sugar mill over there, so you also get some of the history of the island. I think you'd really find it interesting."

"That sounds really good. We don't have anything planned tomorrow, just hanging out here. We'd be happy to go to St. John with you."

"Before you say yes, I suggest you call your wife and make sure it's okay with her. Do you have your mobile phone with you?"

Earl nodded yes, searched around in his pockets for a few minutes, whipped out his flip-phone, then got up and went over to the entrance where the noise from the bar wasn't so loud. He dialed, spoke into the phone for a few minutes, then returned to the table with a big smile.

"She said she'd be happy to go with you to St. John tomorrow, and sounded quite enthusiastic about going. She also told me to get my butt back to the room, so we can get a good night's rest."

"I was about to tell you the same thing," Ricky said, "and make sure you keep that aloe on tonight. I don't want to have to take you to the emergency room here," he added with a laugh. "That would really be quite an experience. And put that aloe in the fridge when you get back."

"So what time do you want us to be ready in the morning?"

"We'll leave the hotel at eight-thirty. Breakfast starts here at seven, and I'll be here then to eat. So if you want to have breakfast here, we can meet at seven, or you can meet me in the lobby at eight fifteen."

"Okay, sounds good. We'll see you in the morning."

Chapter Three

C hapter Three

The next morning, Ricky arrived at the dining room on the beach at ten minutes to seven. The sun had already broken the horizon, but a few puffy, cotton clouds half-way across the top of it, gave the impression of a golden seascape as it sat on the clear, blue water of Sapphire Bay.

The morning breakfast staff was preparing for the early morning meal. A few guests of the hotel were already seated and waiting for the food to be served. Ricky looked around to see if Earl had come in yet, apparently he hadn't. As he was taking a seat, a handsome woman who looked to be in her late thirties, dressed in navy cotton shorts and a pale blue "American Paradise" t-shirt, with a large straw bag slung over one shoulder, came up to him.

"Hi, are you Mr. Brin?" she asked bending over the table.

"Good morning; yes I am," Ricky answered.

"Hi, I'm Marjean, Earl's wife, and he asked me to meet you for breakfast. He said he'll see us in the lobby when we're loading up for our trip."

"Nice to meet you, Marjean. Do sit down. So how is Mr. Earl feeling? I hope his sun burn is better."

"Yes it is, that aloe stuff you gave him really worked well. He's still a little red, but much better than yesterday."

"Glad to hear that. I was afraid that he wouldn't be able to go on our trip because of it."

"I think he'll be fine as long as he doesn't spend much time in the direct sun."

"Well good to hear that, I think he'll really enjoy our little trip."

The servers came to the various tables with steaming coffee kettles, poured the dark liquid into cups, and then proceeded to take orders. Ricky and Marjean both ordered scrambled eggs with whole-wheat toast, and orange juice.

"So, Earl has been telling me about some of the topics you guys have been discussing in your conversations. I think it's great. I don't think he's given serious thought to that stuff since he was in college. Religion and race and social differences. I don't think too many of his friends discuss these kinds of topics. He really seems to be enjoying your little talks, and I think it's important to always be aware of those areas."

Ricky took a sip of his coffee, then carefully put the cup down.

"Why do you think it's important to discuss these social topics?"

"Well they're around us all the time, whether we pay attention to them or not, so I think it's good to be aware, especially of the more controversial ones, like race and religion."

"Do you guys talk about it much?"

"Not as much as we should. I often feel like when our kids ask about it, we should discuss it more, and on a deeper, maybe even historical level."

"How do you mean?"

"I mean we shouldn't be afraid to go back to slavery, where racist attitudes towards blacks started. And then to the Jim Crow years when whites, especially in the south, treated blacks terribly. We seem to be afraid to talk about it, and even though blacks and whites living together has gotten better, racism is still around."

The server brought breakfast, and refilled the half-empty coffee cups. They both sipped their coffee first, and then started buttering their toast. Ricky took a bite of egg and toast off his fork, followed by another sip of his coffee. He cleared his throat and looked at Marjean.

"How do you think people become racist?" he asked her.

"Earl was right, you sure know how to get to the point. But to answer your question, I think more than anything else they learn it. They learn it probably mostly from their parents, and other adults around them when they're very young. And it's not something definite they're told at one time. A lot of it is just observing how these people act towards people of another race, or hearing what they say. Sometimes just little things, like appearance or dress, or speech, how the other race sounds. Kids pick things up quickly. They're like sponges."

"Do you think there were many kids who were racist when you were growing up?"

"Yes. I think a lot of kids I knew who lived in Oklahoma back then thought they were better than other people because they were white and the others weren't."

"Sorry, sorry, sorry, " Ricky said suddenly. "I didn't mean to get into a heavy conversation like this, especially so early in the day. I wanted to ask you about Oklahoma and how you enjoyed living there and going to college there. And here I am asking you about racism on your vacation. At least it's not religion." They both laughed at this.

"I had a feeling we would have this kind of conversation, because Earl told me about some of the topics you guys touched on. I was a little surprised at first, because I know Earl doesn't seem to like getting into these conversations but I think he needs to, especially since, as I said, we're also raising three children. And they do ask questions."

"It's good to hear you say that. So many people are uncomfortable talking about society's rules, so they try to ignore them, which of course leads to ignorance and stupidity. Unfortunately it also leads to real-life consequences, especially for the people who bear the brunt of the discrimination."

"You know when I grew up in Tulsa we had busing, which caused all kinds of problems, especially between blacks and whites. I don't think there was much outward animosity before busing, but once it started people were really mean to each other."

"In many cases the silent kind of racism is the worse. At least when it's loud you know what you're fighting for and who's against you."

"It's funny," Marjean said, "but as a kid growing up I never thought Tulsa was a racist or even prejudiced place. I never thought I was better than people of different races, and besides the black people living there, we also have a lot of American Indians in the state. I never came into contact with different races very often, but when I did, I was always polite and didn't think it was a big deal."

"Well let me ask you this. Did you have black people living in a different section of the city than whites, because that's one of the greatest indicators of racism?"

"Well actually now you mention it, we did. Blacks lived on the north side of Tulsa, and whites on the south."

"Did you also have railway tracks running across where the division was?" Ricky asked with a smile.

"I'm sure they did at some point," Marjean replied.

"So how did you feel about busing?"

"Well I was still pretty young, eleven or twelve, and also I went to a private school. But I had some older cousins in public high school who hated it, and I believe their parents actually went to demonstrations outside the school district offices to protest it."

"When you were older, say by the time you went to college, did you understand why the concept of busing came up, and why there were laws supporting it?"

"Oh, definitely. I got to know several black students quite well in college, and understood their predicament. I also minored in sociology, and had several classes relating to the struggle of minorities, and in particular, African Americans. Busing was an attempt to really desegregate schools. Even though the Supreme Court ruled in nineteen fifty-four that schools had to be de-segregated, there was still a lot of segregation because of where blacks and whites lived. In the bigger cities, blacks lived in the downtown areas, the inner city as it was called, and whites lived in the suburbs."

"So you were much more socially aware than Earl was."

"Yes, I was and still am. And that's a good word 'aware'; it's not like he didn't know all these feelings and attitudes existed, it's just that he didn't want to get involved with them and work out how he really felt about people who were and still are discriminated against. But you've obviously piqued his interest and I'm happy for that, because these acts of racial or cultural discrimination are real, and we should know how we feel about them, and maybe try to understand how it got that way."

"I hope I'm not spoiling your breakfast with all this talk," Ricky said. "Eat up, it's delicious, and you're going to need your strength for our little outing on St. John."

"You're not spoiling my breakfast in the least, and yes it does taste good. But to be honest, I'm enjoying talking to you. I get the feeling this is something you do often with visitors to the island that you meet."

"Yes, you're right. I do try to engage in conversation with visitors I meet when they're willing to engage. Some are very uncomfortable talking about race and other social issues, but it gives me a good idea about how my fellow Americans think."

"And that's another thing, we forget that you guys are American too. We think you're some kind of exotic islanders, who live in a totally different manner from us, and that's not true at all. We have a lot in common."

"We certainly do have a lot in common. I'm as American as you are."

"So in school, I presume the kids say the pledge of allegiance like the kids back in the...I mean on the Mainland. Had to correct myself there." She smiled and sipped her coffee.

"They certainly do, and after school they play football and basketball and baseball, like the kids on the Mainland. And some of them get athletic scholarships, and a couple of them have played in the major leagues, professionally."

"That's very interesting. And we think people here are so different from us just because we come here on vacation. Shows how naive we are back on the Mainland."

"We're all naive," Ricky said with a big smile, "until we take the time to understand and maybe even learn how the world works. I think too many of us take the rules we live by for granted and never question them, and unfortunately we all cause a lot of unhappiness, maybe even cruelty to others when we act and react without thinking."

"I think you're so right, Mr. Ricky. Are you sure you're not a college professor?"

"Well, I have done some teaching, but only in high school and Sunday school."

"Your students are lucky to have someone like you."

"Why, thank you, Marjean. I appreciate those kind words." He paused for a moment, rubbed his chin and then continued. "So tell me something. Have you and Earl been to many places in the Caribbean on vacation. He told me about Puerto Rico and maybe the language problem, but have you been other places?"

"Let's see, we went to Jamaica, and Antigua. Why?"

"Well what I'm getting at, is how do you feel being around so many black people? I'm sure you're around some African Americans in Oklahoma, but those islands you mentioned have a majority black population. So for example, when you arrive at the airport in Antigua and you see mostly black people; do you feel uncomfortable?"

"You know, I've never thought of it. It's just Antigua; which probably means I don't feel uncomfortable at all."

"You're probably right. What about if you were around that many Black Americans in Oklahoma?"

"Hmmm, that's a very, very interesting question. I have to think about that."

The breakfast area was filling up with visitors, and many of them bid Ricky good morning, by name, or waved to him, or gave him a little bow. Marjean was quite surprised at how many of the guests knew him.

"Almost all of them seem to know you. Where do you find the time to get to know so many of them, plus do your business?"

"Well, it's part of my business. I show them the island, but I also talk about it a lot to make it interesting. Besides all the marketing they may have seen or read about the place, I think it's important for them to get a local perspective, maybe with some history thrown in."

"Do you also talk about the subject matter that we've been talking about?"

"Very rarely, and only to a few people I consider special. And Earl and yourself, in my opinion, are special. The subject matter is way too sensitive to be discussed in a general manner to a lot of people."

"Well that's nice that you think we're special. Incidentally, I thought about that hypothetical question you asked me about being more comfortable around black people on the Island than on the Mainland, and I think I have to admit that I would be more comfortable around blacks here."

"What about me? Do you feel uncomfortable around me?" he asked with a smile.

"Not in the least."

"Good."

"But in a way I don't really think you're black, or African American. You're very dark, like many black people I've seen, but you don't have a round nose or thick lips, and even though your hair is curly, it's not really kinky. And then you don't have much of an accent, at least you don't use it when you're talking to me. Your accent is very standard. Most black people on the Mainland that I've listened to have a 'black accent,' and the Jamaican blacks definitely have a very, very strong accent. You know that was the first island I ever visited, and I thought that everyone in the Caribbean spoke like that."

"Thank God they don't," Ricky said with his big smile, again, flashing his very white teeth. "I mean I enjoy listening to my Jamaican friends, but it would be a bit much if we all spoke like that. You know, you're very observant, Mrs. Francis. You should be a professor of Sociology, or Anthropology, dealing with ethnicity and culture. Maybe when your kids graduate from high school you should go back to college."

"Wouldn't I be too old?"

"Not at all. I think that's the best time for higher education. You have the incredible experience of raising children, and still have a lot of youth and energy left."

"I'll have to think about that."

"The truth is that the vast majority of people we call black, especially on the Mainland, are actually part white."

Marjean raised her eyebrows and leaned back, but didn't say anything.

"The white men who owned and worked on the plantations, couldn't keep their hands off the female slaves. They sired many, many children. And even though they called them black or more accurately back then, the N word, they were actually creating a significant mixed- race population."

"I've never given that much thought, but I guess technically you're right. That's why so many black people on the Mainland, aren't really black at all, and are different shades of brown, some quite light-skinned. And yet we identify them all as black, without really thinking about it."

"It's amazing how many areas of life we take for granted and don't really think about them. The conditioning we get in our early years is extremely strong. We all accept it and rarely question it. The ability to examine these supposed facts and rules that we're taught by our parents, is what I believe social education is all about."

"So I guess it was the same for the female African slaves, in the Caribbean and other places where they were."

"Yes, there was definitely the same behavior by the white owners and managers on the plantations here, but there was one difference from the U.S. plantations."

"How so?" she asked brimming with interest.

"Well when the white European men came to the Caribbean, unlike the Mainland, it was still very remote and primitive. So, they didn't bring a lot of white women with them. There was still a lot of disease, some of which they brought, like small pox, which wiped out a lot of the native people, but in some areas, malaria was still very prominent, and killed off a number of Europeans. But the men who got through it and stayed, also wanted to have families, so they got together with the half-white females, and their children who would be a quarter black and three-quarters white, would start to look like white kids. Then the next generation of females who mated with white men would have a number of kids who could look totally white. So in a way, the plantation owners genetically engineered their own white women in the New World."

"That seems pretty drastic. I mean I can see the women being raped by the white men, but to think that they had the where-withal to genetically engineer the race they wanted is another thing."

"Mixed-race families do weird things in this part of the world to keep their ethnicity a certain way. But let me put it another way. These guys knew that if they had sex with a slave-woman and she had a daughter, she, the daughter would have a fairly light completion, maybe some European facial features, but with kinky hair. Then if another white guy had sex with that girl, and if she had a daughter, that daughter would probably have straight or slightly curly white hair and either a white or slightly brown complexion. Now if this girl had a daughter with another white male, her daughter would probably look completely white. And it didn't take long. After twelve to fifteen years, you would have females who didn't look very black at all."

Marjean was staring at him, open mouthed. "You've really thought about this a lot, haven't you?"

"Yes, when you're mixed-race, you tend to think about this stuff."

"So what's your ethnicity?"

"I'm about forty percent black, fifty percent white, and ten percent Native American, or Indian as that idiot Columbus called the native people he encountered in the area. And the white blood I have is French. A number of French families started coming to St.Thomas in the late eighteen hundreds and settled here. They came from the island of St. Barth's, which is a French colony. In terms of race, they were white, and most of them never inter-married with non-whites, but a few did, so some of us are mixed."

"It's amazing that you have all these mixtures in such a small place."

"Yes, most of the people on St. Thomas identify as being black, including me, but the reality is that we have quite a cosmopolitan island."

"So do you speak French?"

"Well my grandparents did most of the time, and my father did when he was young, but not my mother. I did a bit when I was very young, but by the time I got to middle-school, I had given it up. As the island became more modern, most of the French stopped speaking their original language, and very few do today. Looking back, I've often wished the language was kept up. It would have been nice to have a second language, especially French."

"Yes, I think it would have been nice to speak another language, and I often wished I did, but it wouldn't take someone as sharp as you very long to pick it up again."

"I don't know about sharp, especially language wise, but it would take time; and with working at my jobs and being a father to my children and a husband to my wife, I'm afraid the time may have passed me by."

"So do you get involved in these social conversations with your wife?" Marjean asked.

"Actually I do. We've been together for a long time, twenty-five years, and it seems that we've been discussing the problems of society in some form, most of that time."

"Did she go to college too?"

"Yes, she was here at U.V. I. at the same time as me. She's a nurse, an R.N."

"So just like Earl and me, you were in college at the same time. That's cool."

"So let me ask you this," Ricky said looking at his watch: he still had fifteen minutes before they had to leave. "When you guys have social conversations, who would you say is more progressive?"

"Without a doubt, it's me. Besides the fact that I've had more classes in social sciences than him, I just think women in general, especially those who have been to college, tend to be a lot more progressive than men." She stopped speaking for a few minutes and silently looked out over the vast, blue, beautiful Caribbean Sea, so calm this February winter morning in its vast magnificence. He could see her grey-blue eyes moisten as she squinted, as though reading a faraway sign. She continued speaking. "It's probably also because women, in general, have been treated so terribly by society. For so many hundreds, maybe thousands of years, even today still, we've been told we're not equal to men, maybe not even equal to the farm animals in some cultures. Those of us who had the opportunity to understand this, often through college, have had to fight so hard for a better place in this world. You know you mentioned society's rules, and how we're taught to be a certain way, not only by the larger society, but by our parents too, and that really rang a bell with me, especially as a woman. It started me thinking about what was expected of me, and it wasn't to be well educated or to have an important profession, or own a business; it was to find a man before a certain age, make sure he married me, have his children, raise them, keep his house clean, and cook the family's meals. And I basically did all of those things."

"Having true freedom and being an individual, is a lot more difficult than most people think. We are a lot more influenced by those laws of society than we realize. We are all definitely conditioned to behave a certain way. I'll tell you one more story about my wife, then we have to leave. I didn't only go to college with my wife, Annette, we've known each other since we were in elementary school. I'm four years older, but I literally used to walk her to school. Our families both lived in the same general area, Frenchtown, and even though both families are mixed with French-European and African blood, hers doesn't have as much African blood as mine, so in general they're a lot lighter complected than mine, and some of them look white. So when Annette and I started getting serious about each other when she was about sixteen, her parents did not want her to marry someone who looked black. So we actually had to put our relationship on hold for about four years, before we decided to get back together and then get married when we were in college. Let me tell you, it was quite the wedding, with all her family and friends pretending to be happy for her, and at the same time wishing I would disappear, or maybe get a lighter complexion."

"That's really interesting. So even on a tiny island like this, you have these little intricacies in your personal relationships. That's really strange to me. Of course I can hardly wait now, to meet Annette."

"I'll try to arrange it. Right now though, we have to be getting ready to leave." Ricky called the waitress over, was about to tell her to put his breakfast on his bill, when Marjean spoke.

"Please allow me to buy you breakfast. That was one of the best conversations I've had in a long time."

"Thank you. Very nice to meet you. We'll all meet in the lobby," Rick said as he got up. "And this would also be a good time to go to the bathroom."

"Yes sir," she said with a smile as he turned and walked out of the dining room.

Chapter Four

C hapter Four

Ricky stopped at the resort front desk, picked up his list of guests for the day's trip, and waited for them to arrive. Five minutes later, Earl walked in the front entrance, in a navy and red t-shirt with "Go Sooners" prominently displayed across his chest, and a small overnight bag hanging from his left shoulder. Ricky looked at him closely, checking to see if the aloe had improved his sunburn. His complexion was still on the red side, but not as bad as the night before.

"Hey Ricky, how you doing? Ah, good morning, I made it. Ready to go."

"Well, good morning, my friend," Ricky replied to Earl. "I must say you're looking chipper this fine day. I trust you had a good night's sleep. I just finished having breakfast with your lovely wife. We had a wonderful conversation. She should be here shortly."

Promptly at eight-thirty, Ricky climbed into the driver's seat of the midnight blue van and slowly pulled out of the Sapphire

Bay Resort and headed for the main gate. There were nine passengers in the converted seats, and Earl was sitting next to him in the front seat.

As Ricky was about to put on his left turn signal in preparation for exiting Sapphire, he heard a voice shouting his name from behind.

"Mr. Ricky, Mr. Ricky, hold up."

Ricky immediately pulled over and stopped the van. A young, black man in his twenties, dressed in khaki slacks, a pink short sleeved shirt and a brown and white striped tie, was at the driver's window. He was breathing heavily from running behind the van.

"Good morning, boss man," the young man said. "I need a favor. Car trouble, I having car trouble, and I need to get to the ferry to St. John. Can you take me to the Dock, chief?"

"Is that you, young Mr. Allen?"

"Yes, sir."

"Haven't seen you for a while. Of course I can take you. Jump in. We're full, but see if you can squeeze in."

Mr. Allen went in the side door, thanked Ricky, said good morning to everyone, and sat next to Peter, one of the two young boys on the trip. Marjean was sitting on the other side.

"Are you ok, young man. You were really running back there. You're pretty fast," she added with a smile.

"I'm ok thanks, a little winded. I couldn't get my car to start, and I recognized Mr. Ricky's van. I have to catch the nine o'clock ferry to get to my office in time for a meeting. I work for the senator from St. John."

"That must be very interesting. Do you like politics?"

"Did I hear you say you're working for my good friend, Senator Riley?" Ricky said in a loud voice from the driver's seat. "Congratulations. If he didn't live in St. John, he would probably be governor. He still might be."

"Yes sir, he's a very good senator."

"We'll be at the dock in about fifteen minutes, folks. Won't be too long a drive," Ricky said in a loud voice as he turned left and drove along Red Hook Road."

Tommy Allen turned to Marjean. "Yes, I do like politics. I didn't realize how much influence politicians have over citizens, through the laws they do or do not create. Incidentally I'm Tommy."

"Marjean. Nice meeting you," she said. "And it's good to see a smartly dressed young man enthusiastic about a serious job in a senator's office. What do you do?"

"I'm a bit of a jack of all trades, everything from office boy to helping draft legislation."

"That's very impressive. And you're from here? St. Thomas?"

"Actually, my parents are originally from St. Kitts, but I was very young when they moved, so I grew up here."

"And you went to college too, I presume."

"Yes, here at U.V. I. for three years, then two years at Florida State. I ended up with a Bachelor's degree in political science."

"Which is why you work for the senator."

Tommy smiled and nodded his head. He then sat back and turned to Peter, sitting quietly next to him.

"So you're enjoying your vacation in the Virgin Islands?" Tommy asked, gently patting the boy's shoulder.

"Yes sir," he answered. "I really love the water and the beaches."

"I did when I was your age too," Tommy replied.

Ricky, his nine guests and Tommy were all aboard the ferry as it slowly pulled away from the Red Hook Dock on its way to the island of St. John, the smallest of the U.S. Virgin Islands, about twenty minutes away. Marjean and Earl were sitting on either side of Tommy as the vessel accelerated. Marjean introduced him and smiled broadly as Earl made a point of saying "good morning" to him.

"This is beautiful. Smell that fresh, salt air, and hardly a cloud in that wonderful sky. And I have to stay in the shade as much as possible because of this confounded sunburn."

"Doesn't look too bad," Tommy said, "but stay in the shade as much as you can. Sunburns are no fun."

"Yes, you're right. So, you work for a Senator. Do you find government and politics at that level interesting?"

"Yes, I do. I've learned that it's very important to be positive and patient in my line of work. It can take a while to pass a law or sometimes add a simple amendment to an existing one, but when you get something passed that you believe will help your fellow citizens, it can be most rewarding."

"That's well said. I guess the patience is what I would struggle with," Earl said.

"Yes, he would," Marjean added.

"If you don't mind me asking?" Earl said. "What's the meeting you're having today? It sounded important."

"Actually it is. The senator and staff are going to be discussing the possibility of having another resort on the island. We're going to be talking with the investors in the resort as well as people from the various government planning offices. Even though it's in the preliminary stage, whenever there's serious talk about having another hotel, our residents are very interested, both pro and con."

"So do you think it's a good idea? Seems like the more the merrier to me. More business, more money to be made."

"I'm not sure where I stand yet. All beaches in the Virgin Islands are public, and a lot of the newer hotel projects don't realize this. So it all depends on how much they're willing to work with what they're allowed. Part of my job right now is issuing press releases about the discussions. If and when we start having formal hearings, the newspapers and t.v. will do most of the reporting."

"So are there a lot of rules or should I say laws that developers have to follow if they want to build a resort in the V.I.? I really wouldn't have thought it would be that big of a deal."

"I don't want to get into a lot of issues here, but you'd be surprised what developers try to get away with when they present the planning board with a project. The beach is always a big deal, as they want to have it private so that they can say their resort is more exclusive, but of course we have a 'public beach for all' law in the V.I. Sometimes they want taller buildings than our codes allow, claiming they can get better views and charge more for a room. Then they want to build smaller rooms to have more guests, and they all want big tax breaks, claiming they're doing a great job for our economy. And those are a few issues in a nutshell that our elected leaders and the various government departments deal with."

"You know, I never thought I'd learn so much on vacation," Earl said shaking his head in wonder and smiling broadly. "I've also been talking to Ricky, and he's like a walking encyclopedia, or a college professor."

"If you've been talking to Mr. Ricky in some detail you've already learned a lot. He is something else, maybe the smartest man I've ever known."

"He definitely sees things in detail that others take for grant-ed. Very interesting fellow."

The engines on the ferry were louder as the boat started to slow down. Ten minutes later Ricky and his group were on the dock. They walked over to the parking lot, said goodbye to Tommy Allen, and started climbing into the borrowed white van that they would be using for the day. Once everyone was comfortable and in their seats, Ricky announced their general itinerary for their outing.

"I hope everyone enjoyed and survived the ferry ride from St. Thomas. The ocean was calm today, and the visibility was extremely clear and went on for a long way. The views were truly wonderful, and I can truthfully tell you that as long as I've lived here, I never get tired of the beautiful scenery. Today we're going to go to Maho Bay to do some swimming and or snorkeling, and of course also get some sun. A word of caution; please be careful in the sun. And even those of you who have good tans and can tolerate the sun better, I urge you to spend some of your time in shaded areas. If you get a severe burn, it can be very, very painful."

"After Maho Bay, we're going to go to the Annaberg plantation ruins. This is a historic site that is maintained by the government, and it allows visitors to appreciate early plantation life in the islands, including the use of chattel slavery."

"Okay, everyone, get comfortable and buckle up. We're on our way."

Chapter Five

C hapter 5

 The van motor turned over quietly, and the vehicle gingerly pulled away from the Cruz Bay dock, on its way to Maho Bay.

Cruz Bay was fairly busy with small businesses and a few houses, but in a few minutes the van was out of town and driving along the north shore road. They passed the famous Caneel Bay resort and were soon driving along close to the shoreline, very little traffic around, with beautiful views of the various bays.

Earl strained to look past Ricky in the driver's seat to view the scenery.

"This is amazing, simply amazing," he said as they drove along.

"It certainly is," Ricky replied. "That's Trunk Bay down there, and the next one is Cinnamon."

"That's quite an impressive young man you gave a ride to."

"Yes, Thomas is pretty sharp. I've known him since he was quite young. I didn't realize he had a position with the senator from St. John. That's a good place for him, he'll get a good feel for how our political system works. It wouldn't surprise me if he became a major leader in our government."

"It seems that everyone I meet from the island who you know, can become a major leader. You must have some serious influence over these young people."

"You're only meeting a few of them. Many don't pay me much attention at all," he said with a smile. "But I truly believe we can make life better, and I try to get the kids I've worked with to believe they can do things to improve how the world works, even if it's just doing a little bit at a time. And sometimes they feel that they're important and can really help make a significant change. And of course, as you know, I'm always willing to share my philosophy with adults too."

"Don't I know it," he said smiling broadly.

"That's Cinnamon Bay," Ricky said, pointing to the clear, sandy beach as he drove by it. "The next one is Maho, we made good time, about twenty minutes. It's a perfect day for the beach; now don't forget what I said about staying out of the sun as much as possible. They have a nice little bar there. You should make that your home base for the day."

"Yes, boss," Earl replied.

A few minutes later Ricky turned left towards the ocean and drove the van through an opening to a sand and dirt covered parking lot. He parked the van then turned around in his seat to face the passengers behind him.

"We're here folks. Maho Bay. There are bathrooms and changing rooms in that little building to the right, and when you're done changing into swimwear you can bring your bags and personal items back to the van. And please remember to use your suntan lotion liberally, and often. We'll meet in the main bar in an hour and a half for lunch, then we'll go on to Annaberg to see the historic ruins. So, everyone enjoy."

"I don't think I'll go in the water, but I'm sure Marjean will," Earl said. "I'll go sit at the bar and take it easy."

"Good thinking, my man. I'll stretch my legs and say hello to a few people, then I'll join you there."

Ricky strolled around the parking lot and spoke briefly with some of the other taxi drivers. He then walked out an open gateway and ambled along the beach as the dryer sand sometimes gave way under his shoes.

"This is a beautiful beach," he heard a voice say behind him. It was Carol who was getting ready to go into the water with her husband, Billy. They were both members of his group.

"It certainly is," he replied. "Enjoy the water. It's a beautiful day to swim and snorkel."

After fifteen minutes of walking he turned around and headed for the bar. As he entered, he recognized a carpenter friend of his from St. Thomas, sitting at the far end of the bar with a bottle of beer in front of him. Big John Banksy had done several projects for him over the years, and the men were good friends.

Big John was originally from Maryland, and had lived in the Virgin Islands for fifteen years.

"Big John, how you doing, brother? Didn't expect to see you over here. You doing some work, or just taking some time off?"

John stood up when he saw Ricky and the two men shook hands warmly, their free hands on the other's shoulder. John was half a foot taller.

"Good to see you Rick. You're looking well. Hard work is definitely agreeing with you."

They both laughed at this comment.

"Actually, I'm doing some renovations on an old house, and we're waiting on some materials to get here. Can I get you a cold one?"

"A light beer would be fine thanks," Ricky answered as he sat down next to Big John.

Ricky looked around momentarily and saw that Earl was sitting two seats to the right of Big John. Next to him was Jimmy, who was in the middle of a deep conversation with Earl. Ricky gave them a little bow of acknowledgment, which they returned with small head-lifting gestures.

"So are you as busy as ever?" Rick asked John. "Still have the two young guys working for you?"

"Actually there are four of them now. I'm becoming a corporation. I can't complain, business is good, but I liked it better when I was on my own. Sometimes I have too many projects going on at the same time. I guess I need to learn how to say no sometimes."

"Well, that's what happens when you're good at what you do. It doesn't take much for word to get around in a small place."

"I guess if you screw up it works the other way too."

"It certainly does."

The music being played at the bar was from the sixties and seventies, and all the customers seemed to be enjoying it. Ricky heard Jimmy say to Earl, "ah, man, this is great,"when the Beatles "Come Together" started to play. Both Ricky and Big John were nodding their heads to the music, with the latter's shoulder-length brown hair sometimes flipping forward into his eyes. The next song was "He ain't heavy, he's my brother", by the Hollies.

About thirty seconds into the song, Jimmy turned to Earl and said loudly. "Ah, this one is really great. The guys in this band were geniuses. This was a great Viet Nam song. All about the great brotherhood among the troops there."

"Were you in Nam?" Big John asked him in his deep voice.

"No, I wasn't, had a medical exemption, bad knees, but two of my closest friends were drafted, and they told me about it."

"Did they make it back?" John asked.

"Yes, fortunately they did. Had one of the biggest welcome home parties for them. They were really good guys. We were all on the basketball team together in high school. That's how I messed up my knees. From what I've heard over the years I was very lucky."

"Yes, you were very, very lucky," Big John said. "I wouldn't wish that experience on my worst enemy."

"Were you there?" Jimmy asked.

"Yes," Big John answered. "I was in Viet Nam."

Ricky placed his hand on his friend's forearm and patted it gently.

"It's okay, I can talk about it," John said softly to Ricky. "It's important for people to have some understanding of what it was all about. But don't worry, I'm not going to get into details here. Just talk about music."

"Do you think you guys did have some success in stopping the spread of communism in the East? I know we were also fighting against it in Cuba, and that seemed to work out well. But Viet Nam has always been more of a mystery to me."

"I think it was a mystery to all of us who served there, but I don't want to get into all of that here. But I will tell you what I think about that song that you like. I've read a lot about people saying what a great anthem it was for my fellow Viet Nam vets, and how it brought us closer together and how we all were willing to lift our fellow troops up and take them to safety if they got shot, and never leave anyone behind."

"Yes, that's what my friends told me," Jimmy said.

"Well, we listened to a lot of music when we weren't on patrol, and even though I'm sure I heard this song, I can't remember thinking anything special about it. When I think about the song now, I don't think the Hollies had any soldiers in mind when they wrote and performed it. I believe they were talking about all of humanity. And wouldn't it be a great thing if we could all help all of our fellow humans instead of fighting and competing against them. So when they sing about his welfare being my concern, and he's not a burden, they're singing about how we should all feel towards one another. The American soldiers shouldn't only feel this way towards their fellow soldiers, but even towards the Viet Cong. Perhaps if we really felt more like this towards each other there wouldn't be any wars. Does that make any sense to you?"

Jimmy nodded but didn't say anything.

The music at the bar had stopped, and the atmosphere for about ten minutes was eerily quiet.

The music started again, with Otis Redding singing "Sitting on the Dock of the Bay". The bar customers started talking again. There was laughter and voices.

"Here's another great oldie," Earl said. "What a great voice."

"Yes indeed. Great voice. Pity he died so young."

"I didn't realize that," Earl said.

"Yeah, he died in a plane crash," Big John added.

"So you really believe that Hollies song was written for all mankind and not the soldiers in Viet Nam?" Jimmy said.

"Yes, I do. I believe it's a lot more universal than one conflict where soldiers fought and died. They have been doing that for thousands of years. The Hollies are asking the questions - Why do we do this? Why do we fight and kill one another? Why don't we help each other instead? John Lennon in his song, 'Imagine' asks similar questions. Imagine all the people living life in peace. All I can say is when you go through the horrors of war, you tend to think a lot about this stuff." Big John leaned back and took a big gulp from his bottle.

"You know, my friend, you may be right. That song really could be about all of us. Can I buy you a beer?"

Big John Banksy nodded in affirmation. "I'd appreciate that," he said.

"By the way, I'm Jimmy." John told him his name and the two men shook hands. "Hope I didn't come across too strong with my comments. It's just that Viet Nam was a pretty big deal to me when I started college back in the day. It affected a lot of people in our country."

"It was a big deal, Jimmy. There was a lot of misinformation and outright lying by the powers that be. As a result a lot of young men died needlessly, on either side. It's one thing to go to war and fight for your country. It's another to not know what the hell you're fighting for, or why. So to go back to the song, wouldn't it be great if we all just looked after each other and didn't feel the need to fight and kill each other?"

"Yes, that would be a great way to live, but unfortunately we humans have constantly been at some war with one another for a long, long time."

The music started again, Blood Sweat and Tears playing "What Goes Up Must Come Down". Several people around the bar knew the words and were singing along.

"So, are you visiting too or do you live here?" Jimmy asked.

"I live here. It's been about fifteen years now, originally from Baltimore. I'm a carpenter. Well, I should say I'm a contractor now, as I have a couple of guys working for me. I live over in St. Thomas, but I'm just starting a job over here. Just waiting on some of the supplies to be loaded on to a ferry so that I can get started."

"So would you say life is a lot different here in the islands than back on the mainland?"

"Sure it's different. It's much smaller than all decent size cities, so it doesn't take long to get to know people, once you move here. But I suppose everyone who lives in a small town knows each other too. But it's not the same here. There's more individuality. It's like you know people, but they don't intrude in your life. Hard to explain if you haven't actually lived here for a while."

"What about the racial situation? Do you ever feel uncomfortable living on an island where the majority of people are a different race? In this case, black."

Big John sipped his beer then cleared his throat. He knew Ricky, who had been quiet for quite a while was listening to him.

"There are many days here that I am not even aware of a racial difference." Out of the corner of his eye he could see Ricky nodding in agreement.

"But it takes a while to get to that stage," John continued. "In the beginning most of us whites who come here from the mainland bring our preconceived ideas with us. But I truly believe that one of the reasons most of us decide to stay is because of how comfortable we feel among people of different races and also cultures. Besides the majority of West Indian Blacks who live here, we also have a large Puerto Rican community, and a sizable group from India."

"Being from New York, as you probably know we have different ethnicities and cultures too, but we have so many more people there, and it's like we have rules as to where people can live and how they should behave and what is accepted and what isn't. These rules are what creates the differences between people. I've lived there most of my life, and I must say, it bothers me."

"You're right, there are rules, and these are probably created and held in place by the people with money and power. Every society has these to a certain extent, but here a lot of the rules are relaxed, and as a result, people are more accepting and don't judge others as harshly as they do on the mainland."

"Sounds like a good place to live, and of course the weather and scenery are amazing."

"Yeah, it is. The only events that upset life in the islands are hurricanes. The storms themselves are manageable, but in an isolated place like this, it takes forever to repair the damage caused by a major hurricane that hits us directly."

"But I'm sure storms that cause damage would be good for your business, being a carpenter."

"I'd much rather do without the extra business and keep life normal. I've seen a number of my good friends suffer a lot of tough times and hardship because of a hurricane. But they are a part of life in the entire Caribbean."

"Like the tornadoes we have in Oklahoma," Earl, who was also listening to the conversation, added.

"Yes, my friend," Big John said and drank some more beer.

"So, everything going well?" he asked Ricky quietly, turning to his left.

"You know me, trying to stay busy."

"I don't know how you manage to do so much and still hold it all together. The taxi driving, the mentorship of the young people, the rehabilitation of the tourists, and then your work with the government. Not to mention your religious-type teaching. I don't know how you do it, and in such a laid back place. I tell you brother, I tip my hat to you."

"Well, it's only laid back if you want it to be, and when you're having a casual drink with someone, you can really get ideas across to them, maybe even change what they believe. I just enjoy it, and really don't see it as work. Of course the government work is different, more about serious decision making, but I've managed to minimize that."

"Are you still the actual assistant commissioner of zoning for the V.I. or have you resigned? I see your name in the paper every now and then, when there's a hearing for a new housing or resort project, but they don't actually say what your position is."

"Well, I'm officially on a leave of absence from the department, but they still call me in whenever they need my input, especially with the larger projects."

"So when you're not listening to multi-million dollar proposals to develop new resorts, you're driving visitors around the island in your taxi van."

"Something like that."

"You're a very different person, Mr Ricky," Big John said with a wide smile.

"Yeah, I must be. My wife reminds me of that all the time."

"I've got to go check on my supplies," John said, pushing his chair back and slowly getting up. He paid his bar bill, thanked Jimmy for the beer, said goodbye to Ricky, then walked out with his slow, wide gait, to the parking lot.

Ricky stood up and moved over to John's chair.

"That's an interesting guy," Jimmy said to him. "I just meet this guy at a bar on a vacation island, and before you know it, I'm discussing the Viet Nam War and race relations."

"Yes, we tend to talk a lot about fairly serious and pertinent subjects here in the V.I. We have a lot of very sensitive and intelligent people, and it makes for some great conversations, especially at bars."

"I would have thought it would be quite the opposite, especially with visitors who are here to relax, enjoy the natural beauty, and take a rest from the serious subjects in the world."

"I don't think we can ever really, completely walk away from the more 'serious subjects of the world' as you put it, once you reach a certain level of education and are aware of them. And the problem is, we see them everywhere. For example, you're walking out on the beach early in the morning with your wife, looking forward to a day of sun, swimming, maybe some snorkeling, and a forty-five year old guy with a limp drags a couple of beach chairs up to you and you sign for them, while remarking to your wife, what a nice guy he is. Another guest who's also there to relax, might see things differently. He may have studied economics or sociology in college, and he would see the situation differently. He might wonder why this gentleman is doing this kind of work, and ask what kind of salary is he making. And is it enough to feed and clothe himself? What about if he's married and has children, can he support them with what he's paid to hand out beach chairs to tourists?"

Jimmy was silent for several minutes. He cleared his throat and attempted to say something once, but then shut up and pushed his head back over the chair.

Earl leaned over and said to Jimmy with a chuckle. "I see you're having a nice chat with our taxi driver. Isn't he interesting?"

"Is he always like this? I mean, I feel like I'm in college again."

"That's our Mr. Ricky. He'll make you think whether you want to or not."

Ricky looked at his watch and decided it was time to get his group together for lunch. He told Earl and Jimmy that he was going out to the beach to bring everyone in for lunch, then got up and briskly walked towards the shimmering white sand and the turquoise ocean.

It took him about fifteen minutes to get the seven members of the group together. Four were in the water, and the two boys were building a sand castle with their father, Luke. They were quite efficient and focused, and the castle was a little masterpiece. Everyone in the group looked at it with admiration as they walked by, drying themselves, as they made their way to the dressing rooms to get ready for lunch.

Fifteen minutes later, they were all seated at the table at the back of the bar; some drinking iced tea from the large jug in the middle of the table, a few drinking beer. Ricky sat at the head of the table with the two boys on one side and their dad on the other.

"So you guys enjoying your tour so far?" he asked the youngsters. "Did you go in the water at all?"

"Yes, we were in for a few minutes," Brandon, the older one answered, "and it was really refreshing, but the sand was nice and firm on the beach, perfect for building a castle, so we decided to build one."

"Well, I must say that's a great sand castle, maybe one of the best I've ever seen. You did a great job," Ricky said.

"Thank you," Brandon replied, "we like to build things and make sure they come out right."

"And what do you do Mr. Luke?"

"I'm a school teacher in Boston, I teach math."

"Ah, a man who understands precision. I should have guessed. You've certainly taught these young men well."

"They've done a lot of this themselves since they were very young. They both want to be engineers. My wife and I just provide the materials for them to work with."

"Well you guys have certainly been a good influence on their education. Do they go to private school?"

"No, just a good Boston Public school. They also both play a lot of baseball and are quite good."

"That's good to hear. I'm a strong supporter of public schools."

When lunch was over, Ricky stood up and announced that they would be leaving shortly on their way to the Annaberg plantation, which the National Park had maintained for a long time.

"It's only about twelve minutes up the hill to Annaberg, and you will see the buildings as they were since the seventeen hundreds. The great irony of Annaberg is that it has one of the most beautiful views in the world, but unfortunately that is weighed against the terrible institution of chattel slavery that was put in place there in order to produce sugar profits. I don't want this to sound like a lecture now, but this is an excellent opportunity for you guys to see, and feel and imagine how a slave plantation was run. Think of it as a learning experience, where you are truly enlightened."

"Sounds good."

Chapter Six

Chapter 6

As they pulled into the Annaberg parking lot, the magnificence of the view became apparent to the entire group. The area the plantation sat on was just above Leinster Bay and several islands could be clearly seen off the coast not far away, including the western end of the island of Tortola, largest of the British Virgin Islands.

Ricky parked the van and got out. He walked up to a slim young man with a dreadlocks hairdo, who was obviously waiting on him, warmly shook hands with him, and gestured to his group. He brought the young man back to the van where most of the passengers were getting out.

"This is Wally, guys. He's going to be our tour guide today. Besides his job as a guide, Wally is also a student at the local university, and has written some excellent papers on the ruins up here, and their historic implications and value."

"Another intellectual," Earl said to Marjean. "Where does he find them on these tiny islands?"

"Amazing," she replied, "it never seems to end."

"Good afternoon everyone," Wally said as he addressed the group. "We're going to follow this path out of the parking lot, around the buildings, and go up to the mill. There's enough room for two abreast, and remember we keep to the left here. Today is a perfect day for viewing the ruins; hardly a cloud in the sky and quite cool. Even though we're in St. John today, I want you to understand that practically every island in the Caribbean, all the way through Central America and a lot of South America operated this way, with their economies based mostly on sugar, and with forced labor forced to provide the necessary work. A few hundred years ago, practically every European country owned islands that perpetuated the institution of slavery. Of course, back then the Virgin Islands were owned by the Danes, but this kind of business was practiced by the English, French, Dutch, Portuguese and Spanish, to name a few. And of course we Americans had our slavery too. Anyway, before I get into this lecture any more, let's go to the mill and see what it actually looked like."

A few minutes later the group was standing in front of the sugar mill tower. It was still in pretty good shape, with most of the outer stones and mortar intact. Once the windmill was built, at the end of the eighteenth century, it provided the power needed to move the wheel in the mill around, which made it easier to grind the cane to produce the juice, that was made into sugar. Few plantations had a powerful windmill like this one, and it made Annaberg one of the most profitable operations in the V.I.

The group took in the view and the plantation for several minutes before Wally spoke.

"Welcome to Annaberg, friends. This was a very profitable sugar plantation, and if you look around, beyond the ruins, you'll see all all the land that was cultivated to produce the most successful crop at the time-sugar. Before we get into the economic and social implications of this enterprise, I'll outline how the process worked. When the slaves arrived at the plantation, they were housed in the slave-quarters. Unfortunately, you can barely make out those buildings today, as they weren't very well constructed and deteriorated rapidly over the years. If you look behind you to the right, to the rubble farthest away from the mill, you can just make out rather vague remains of the quarters. Sugar cane is technically in the grass family, so there's no specific planting and harvesting season like most other crops. Sugar also takes a full year to ripen, so the planting takes place around the same time as the harvesting, which makes for a tremendous amount of hard work."

"So now to summarize the process: the bottom part of the cane stalk is cut off from the ripe cane and placed on the ground under a thin layer of soil, in the open field. This can take a couple of months, depending on the size of the field and the amount of slaves. During the next ten to twelve months, the plants all have to be tended to. A lot of this is dealing with the tropical insects that could wipe out the crop, so the slaves had to be always viligant. Rodents and snakes also had to be dealt with. The cane also required a substantial amount of water and when it didn't rain much or there was drought, the slaves had to bring barrels of water by hand up from the creek."

"Once the cane had grown to full size which could be twenty feet and was ready for harvest, the slaves would cut the individual canes about a foot from the bottom, bundle them and load them unto carts, pulled by oxen or mules, and take them to the mill, where they would be crushed to get the juice out. This had to be done within two days of the harvest or the cane juice would begin to harden, reducing the yield. This was the most dangerous part of the operation, as there was a lot of boiling water in a small area with several giant metal wheels crushing the cane that had to be fed by hand. They suffered a lot of serious injury as often this went on for twenty-four hour periods. The cane juice was then cooled and turned into a thick, liquid-like sludge, and some of it was used to be crystallized into sugar, and the rest was turned into molasses. From this the sugar cane could be distilled into rum."

"That, my friends, was the basic process of cultivating sugar on this plantation. Of course the next step was shipping most of it to the Europeans, who paid a small fortune for it.

So, hopefully you all have a pretty good idea of how the journey from cane to sugar and rum worked."

Ricky, beaming like a proud father, put his two hands together, which signaled to the group to do the same. They applauded gently for a few minutes, then Wally spoke again.

"Thank you, folks. I appreciate the gesture, but I want you to know that it's always difficult to explain to people how sugar was produced without saying something about the social horrors of slavery, but I want to try to keep this about the physical process.."

"I know it must be hard for you, Wally, but you did a great job explaining a complex process in a very short period of time," Marjean said.

"What about other crops?" Jimmy asked. "Did the owners grow other products for their consumption? I know there was some coffee grown, and the weather is great for fruit and vegetables."

"At first they tried to grow several products, and coffee was certainly a big one, but once they realized the great profits that could be gained from sugar, it became all sugar, at least here in St. John. Now, there were a few local farms that provided some food for the owners, but much of their food was imported from Europe. Of course the slaves had to grow their own food. They were given small plots close to the quarters to tend. The owners had no intention of going to any extra expense to feed them. It was okay under normal conditions, but if there was a drought and their plants died, they would have little to eat, and some, especially the older ones actually died from starvation."

"Slavery was certainly terrible," Jimmy said, "thank God we've come a long way. In our country we were fortunate to have a man like Abe Lincoln who had the strength and conviction to end it."

Ricky turned around and looked at Jimmy. "You're right about Mr. Lincoln," he said. "He was a brave man with strong principles that probably ended up costing him his life. He lived at a very difficult time and almost lost a third of his country. The Civil War was a terrible experience for millions of Americans. There were a lot of confused people in our country at that time."

"What do you mean confused?"

"What I mean is that a lot of Americans believed they had the right to kidnap or capture people from another country and ship them back to our country to work as slaves for the rest of their lives."

"But we weren't the only ones that did this. We're standing in a place where another country did the same thing. It's just what a lot of them did at that time."

"Other countries didn't claim to believe that 'all men were created equal' as we did. When we put words like that in our Declaration of Independence and then act in a manner completely opposite, it makes us hypocrites, and other countries see this."

"You're right as usual," Marjean said with a laugh, trying to lighten the suddenly serious mood of the group. "It's definitely hypocrisy."

"One other thought I have about hypocrisy, if you would bear with me. The British owned many islands in this part of the world that had slavery, but the practice was halted in 1834. In our country, we maintained this terrible way of life until 1865; thirty years later. And it took a horrible war and the deaths of over a quarter of a million Southerners, who were willing to die to maintain slavery. Chattel slavery which lasted over two hundred and fifty years, was truly the greatest stain on America. Anyway, here's Wally again. Sorry my man, I got social. Didn't mean to jump in."

"Oh, that's okay Mr. Ricky. I know how passionate you can get sometimes when talking about how man has treated his fellow man throughout history." He turned towards the group. "My friends, I do these presentations several times a week in the tourist season, and it's never easy, especially for someone of my ethnicity, but I love to teach and educate people, and the one thing we should all try to take away from a slave plantation is how far humans have come from those times. We can still be better, but we've made some giant steps."

"We certainly have," Billy said. He and his wife, Carol were the youngest couple. He was an ambulance driver In Pennsylvania and Carol ran a physician's office. " You gave a very good presentation. I'm sure we all have a better understanding of how sugar plantations worked. Thank you."

"And we also thank you," Luke said. "My boys understood everything quite clearly, including the horrible institution of slavery.My wife and I both believe the boys are old enough to develop an understanding of significant historical events. Sometimes in school, events and past human behavior are whitewashed and oversimplified for them. We want them to understand the truth about life, so that they can hopefully always be aware of making it better. And with that in mind, you did an excellent job in your talk."

"Thank you, sir. I wish more parents were as open minded as you when raising their children."

"Now folks, we're going to walk around the plantation to get a closer look at some of the other buildings. These will give you a strong sense of the reality of history, of what actually went on here. About a hundred and seventy years ago, the owners, overseers and slaves stood exactly where we are now. The first place we're going to look at is the boiling room, where the daily non-stop boiling of the crushed cane took place. When we walk around I want it to be fairly informal. I'll give you some information, but I want you to feel free to present any ideas you have on the subject, so let's go."

They slowly walked over to the well-preserved boiling room, when Earl spoke.

"You know what's amazing and also sad, is we look at this room, knowing all the hard work and misery that went on here, and then we look to the left, out over the bay, and we see one of the most magnificent views we've ever seen. The juxtaposition between the two is really incredible."

"That's a phenomenon that never fails to hit me every time I'm here," Wally replied.

"If you're a religious person it's like you're seeing heaven and hell," Jimmy said.

"Oh, Jimmy that's a bit much, don't you think?" his wife added.

"No, he's right ma'am, it is like heaven and hell. Slavery wasn't only about the terrible way you were treated physically, it was also about the way you were stripped of every shred of human dignity. And on top of everything you had to endure this your entire life. Like being deep under water in the ocean, and having no possible way of getting to the surface. If this wasn't hell, it had to be pretty close."

"So this is where the really important work took place. The boiling of the crushed cane. I guess this determined how much sugar they actually got," Marjean said.

"You're absolutely right ma'am. This part of the operation was quite technical. The tester had to determine exactly when to stop boiling. If it was too long they would end up with too much molasses, and they couldn't make sugar from that, only rum. And even though they could make a little money from the rum, that's not what they wanted. They wanted sugar, which most of Europe was addicted to."

"And you said during the harvest they would often boil twenty-four hours a day."

"Yes, ma'am, the conditions were brutal. Standing next to large copper vats, getting burned and inhaling clouds of cane vapor all day."

"How long did this last?" Marjean asked.

"As long as two months."

"It's amazing how well these two buildings survived. They're still in pretty good shape, with a lot less deterioration than the others around. I mean these walls are solid," Marjean said patting the brick walls.

"The plantation owners made sure that they double-walled and really reinforced the important buildings. This is the general trend at all the plantations I've been to. The tower where the cane was crushed and the rooms where it was boiled were the heartbeat of the operation."

"Where was the owner's house? Did that deteriorate? I imagine it would have been built out of wood."

"The big house was built out of wood," Wally replied. "It wasn't that close to the plantation, and built up on a hill. Apparently it was still being used when slavery ended here in eighteen forty-eight, first as a Masonic lodge and then as a boy's boarding house. Then in nineteen sixteen the island took a direct hit from a major hurricane and the house was completely destroyed. It's a pity. If they were able to restore it, that would have enhanced the historical value of the plantation even more."

The group walked around the three heavy stone buildings talking softly to each other. They also walked through the part of one building where the overseers had their quarters. Wally identified the area for them as he walked along.

Ricky was in a group with Earl, Marjean, Jimmy and Kathy.

"This is really something special," Marjean said. "It's like being in a college course. Wally's great; he's like the professor you could listen to all day."

"I guess I should have paid more attention in U.S. history," Earl said. "I always knew slavery was bad, but I never realized how much the slaves really went through. I imagine the cotton plantations operated the same way. I guess I was too involved in learning about business to pay too much attention to history."

"My good friend, Earl, what your professors didn't teach you is that plantations and slavery were all about business. It was one of the most profitable businesses in the history of the world. You had a product that you knew was profitable, especially in Europe where the upper class had a lot of money. The plantation owners could make excellent profits by paying wages to workers, but they were greedy and wanted to make even more so they found slavery, which wasn't free labor, but it was extremely cheap.So you had a great product, cheap labor and big profits. Economics one oh one. And they were making so much, some were willing to sacrifice the lives of hundreds of thousands of Southern young men, while also being willing to destroy their own country."

"How do you always seem to come up with the right answers and also questions to these situations? I think I'm making some simple, mundane, comment to you, and you turn it into an important event." Earl spoke slowly.

"I wouldn't say I have the right answers to everything, but I've always paid attention to how the world has worked, and it's amazing how many situations fit the same formula."

"You're an amazing taxi driver, Mr. Ricky. You have all this historical background and you get all this other knowledge from driving visitors around in your van. I don't mean to sound sarcastic, but what you're saying is just common sense. Everyone knows that plantations were profitable, but a lot of people believe the Civil War was all about state's' rights, not slavery," Jimmy said.

"Many people have said that, especially Southerners, but I've always felt it was only an excuse to justify slavery. I don't believe that many people would have been willing to die for state's' rights. But if that's your opinion I can understand why you feel that way. Maybe we'll be able to talk about it some more later."

Ricky looked over at Wally who pointed to the exit of the boiling room. Ricky nodded, and then told the group the rest of the itinerary. They would walk over to the dungeon, then down to the ruins of the slave quarters, then stop at the bar for refreshments and reflection, then back to the van.

"So what was the dungeon used for?" Jimmy asked as the group walked along the dirt path towards it.

"It was used to punish the slaves who misbehaved, as judged by the overseers. This could be anything from oversleeping, usually because of sickness, to being injured or burnt in the sugar production and causing the operation to have to slow down, or it could be a female who was fighting too hard as she was being raped. More than anything it was used to make the slaves so afraid they would do whatever the overseers required. Oh, before I forget, some of the worst punishments were visited on slaves who were engaged in the most forbidden act on the plantation. Can anyone tell me what that was?"

"Attempting to escape from the plantation," Jimmy said.

"No, that was bad but not the worst," Wally replied.

"Stealing food from the great house," Marjean suggested.

Wally smiled at her and shook his head. "Anyone else?"

"Learning to read and write?" Luke said.

"Correct," Wally said. "That was the greatest crime on every slave plantation. The last thing any owner wanted was for their slaves to become educated. This could lead to serious revolts and other violent actions by them."

Some of the group peered into the dungeon. A few actually went in. They were all surprised by how small the dimensions were inside. Marjean attempted to go in but stopped at the entrance. Earl went up to her and placed an arm around his wife's shoulders When they turned around one could see a few tears running down her face. When Ricky saw this he quickly went over to her.

"It's okay, Marjean," he said gently. "Many people who come here have an emotional reaction to the cruelty that took place where they're actually standing. I cried for days the first time I saw the dungeon."

"You alright, hon?" Earl asked.

"I'll be fine. It just all hit me at one time when I looked in. I'll be fine."

The group left the dungeon and walked down to the ruins of the slave quarters. A few of the shacks had stone foundations, and this was all that was left of where five hundred slaves lived at any given time during slavery. Wally went up to the largest stone and placed the palm of his left hand on it, while looking up to the sky. He appeared to be saying a silent prayer and was soon back among the group.

"Well, folks, this is our last stop today. Approximately five hundred enslaved people lived in this area. Unfortunately, most of the housing has completely deteriorated, but we still have these stone foundations to remind us. The area behind the housing was where the food was grown. It was okay except when there was a drought, when some literally starved to death."

"Was there any medical help for them?" Carol asked.

"Very little," Wally replied. "There usually was someone who used some form of herbal medicine, but they were limited as to all the herbs they needed. There was always a mid-wife. A lot of infants were born during slavery. Besides encouraging the male slaves to sire a lot of children, the owners and overseers constantly mated with the younger female slaves and produced a plethora of mulatto children. This was especially true in the U.S, where most black people are part white."

"So were these female slaves just raped, like on a constant basis?" Carol asked.

"One of the worst aspects of being a female slave was that you could be raped at any time by the white bosses, day or night, night or day."

"That's really terrible," Carol said. "I didn't realize it happened so often."

"So, that's why so many black people a have a lighter complexion than others, they're really part white," Katherine said.

"I thought you knew that," Jimmy said to his wife. "We've got a whole bunch of light-skinned black people in New York. Some are practically as white as us."

"I know we do. I guess I just never thought about it."

"I bet you'll think about it some more after visiting this plantation," Marjean added with a smile.

"Do you think that black people think about slavery all the time?" Jimmy whispered to Marjean. "I mean, when do they move on? This is something that ended a long time ago. I mean other bad things also happened in the world, like wars or locking people up without due process, but people do get over it and move on. People sometimes make mistakes."

"Maybe you should ask someone who's black, but I think Wally already heard you."

"I don't mean to eavesdrop, Mr. Jimmy," Wally said, smiling sweetly, "but do you want me to answer your question?"

"Sure, may as well get as much information on this topic as we can."

"I can't speak for all black people, only the ones I know, and I can tell you that practically every one thinks about the effects of the institution of slavery every day of their lives in some form or other. I have a very intelligent sociology professor in college, and he believes that in the Americas the effects of slavery have always been a part of the very air we breathe, and that everyone is and was deeply aware of it, whether they wanted to be or not. When he speaks of the historic and social ramifications of the institution, particularly in the United States, he is absolutely incredulous that it lasted so long after the founding of the country. He believes that this institution shouldn't have been ended by President Lincoln, but by President Washington. This should have been in the very first article of the Constitution, especially after Mr. Jefferson made such a proud reference to all men being equal. I remember during one class my professor was visibly upset during a lecture, constantly repeating 'how could they let this go on so long? how could they let this go on so long? You see Mr. Jimmy, from the very beginning of our country this was the elephant in the room, and it has never completely left."

"That's quite a speech, Wally. You know a part of me feels that having to listen to what you just said is like the last thing a guy wants to hear on vacation when he should be relaxing and enjoying his holiday. But on the other hand, I did know we were coming to a historic site where slavery existed, and I realize how impossible it is for one to feel that he can relax around such a terrible experience."

"And you're the one who asked the question," Marjean said.

"Yes, you're right," Jimmy agreed.

"I hope I didn't offend you, Mr. Jimmy. But my job here is to be informative and honest, and I would answer your question the way I do everyone's, no matter what your ethnicity is. Slavery was slavery and most black people are very much aware of it all the time."

Wally looked at his watch, nodded at Ricky, and told the group they would be going down to the bar, which was next to the parking lot where they came in. They walked up the hill away from the slave quarters, and then down a slight decline on the way to the lot. Ricky hung back to make sure everyone was accounted for, then he stayed at the back of his group as they headed on. He noticed someone else was walking very slowly and had dropped back to be near him. It was Billy, Carol's husband.

"Hi, Mr. Billy," Ricky said to him. "Hope you're enjoying the tour."

"Oh yes, it's very informative and interesting. I know I haven't said anything so far, but I have been taking it all in, and Carol and I have discussed it. There is one thing I wanted to ask you, but I didn't want to do it in front of the others as it might be a stupid question and Wally could turn it into one of his lectures. But this is something I've heard from friends of mine and I really didn't understand the concept, or even the comparison. But I usually hear about it from people who don't believe that racism exists, or that it holds back black people. Now Carol and I have never believed that, and I think we've always been aware of people who were unfortunately negatively affected by racism, especially people who had inadequate educations because of their race, and were put at a disadvantage in life from their early years."

Ricky smiled and shook his head. "What's this thing you want to ask me, Mr. Billy?"

"Well, these people say that a lot of slavery existed in the world long before the United States came into being and they agree that all slavery was bad, but it was no different than what we had on our plantations. They say even the American Indians had slaves. Anyway, their whole belief is that slavery has been over for a long time and maybe we should let it go and look to the future more, and move on."

Ricky was silent when he heard what Billy wanted to talk about. He put his hands in his pockets and looked at his shoes as he walked along. He took a deep breath and then spoke.

"Have you ever heard of Jim Crow, Mr. Billy?"

"Yes, I have. I believe it was a term used to describe the way blacks were treated, especially in the South."

"You're right. Jim Crow rules, laws, customs, all started shortly after slavery ended in eighteen sixty-five. Black Americans, and notice I say Americans, were not allowed to drink at the same public drinking fountains as White Americans, weren't allowed to use the same public restrooms, weren't allowed to eat at the same restaurants or stay in the same hotels or travel in the same train cars etcetera. There was also a lot of violent behavior heaped on Black Americans in the form of burning their houses and also lynchings. This of course, was carried out by organizations like the Ku Klux Klan. Are you with me?"

"Yes, sir. I'm with you. Those were terrible times."

"The point I'm making here, is that these terrible times lasted for about a hundred years, and even though this happened mostly in the South, it was also in other parts of the country, and white people in these places didn't do much to try to stop it. I believe that if blacks in the South simply accepted the way life was and moved on, we would still have Jim Crow today. Of course this led to the Civil Rights movement, which made many Americans more aware of the problem and helped effect some changes for the better. Racism may be better than it used to be, but we have to always fight against it in order to ever come close to fulfilling the promise of this country."

"I totally get your point. It's definitely something to be constantly aware of."

"Now, to your question about other people owning slaves. For centuries when two armies went to war, the losing soldiers would often be captured and taken back to the city or country where the victors were from, and forced into slavery. If they went to war again, and the other side won, it would do the same thing. Some Native American tribes did the same thing. They captured their living adversaries after a battle and brought them back into forced labor. But this was the consequence of losing in war. Chattel slavery was completely different. Ships were sailed to Western Africa, and men, women and children were captured and taken back to the New World, where they were sold as actual property. They belonged to the owners who possessed them in every way you can possibly imagine; total and legal ownership, according to the laws of their country.They were chattels and this was chattel slavery. Never in the history of mankind had anything like this ever happened. A number of European countries and the United States, decided to go to the continent of Africa and capture over twelve million people and sell them into slavery for no other reason than to make money. And remember, approximately two million of the slaves never completed the trip, as they perished during the crossing. Now, every form of slavery is terrible and cruel, but to compare the relatively random acts of human capture to the systematic, methodical, structured machinery involved in chattel slavery, then you're comparing apples to coconuts. Very often people who think like this are trying to say that because there was slavery before, the enslavement of Black Americans wasn't so bad, and maybe we just need to forget about and move on."

"You explain that amazingly well, Mr. Ricky, thank you. I'll certainly think more about it than I did before. The way you formulate the entire, terrible institution means you've given it a great deal of thought. Did you go to college too?"

"Yes, I spent some time here at the local college."

"Must be a good school. You guys really know what you're talking about."

"Thank you, Mr. Billy. You know when you said you'd think about it some more, that's all that's asked of us as intelligent humans, instead of taking things for granted. Now let's have a cold drink before our drive back to the ferry." Ricky had an arm around Billy as he spoke.

"Sounds good."

Chapter Seven

C hapter 7

By the time Ricky and Billy got to the little stained wooden building with the green roof, the others were sitting in the shade on the patio outside, being served by the waitress. Ricky and Billy took a seat at the table where Carol was sitting, and both ordered ice teas and leaned back in their chairs.

"You know we didn't walk around that much back at the ruins, but I must admit I feel rather tired, as if we did."

"It's all mental tiredness," his wife replied with a smile, "Mr. Ricky and Wally gave us quite a history lesson, and I believe we all got a lot out of it."

"Well, I'm glad to hear that," Ricky said. "We want you guys to relax and take it easy on your vacation, but we also believe if we can use some of the resources of the islands to enlighten you, that's also a legitimate part of your visit."

"We certainly didn't expect it to be this serious, but we are grateful for everything we learned. I think it's a tragedy that so much of this has never be taught in high school. I believe if it was, race relations may have started to improve a long time ago."

"Yes, I think you're probably right. By the way, where are you guys from? I know it's somewhere in the northeast."

"We're from Pennsylvania, just outside of Philadelphia."

"Ah, our nation's birthplace. And what do you do if you don't mind my asking?"

"We're both in the medical field. I'm an ambulance driver and Carol works at the front desk in a physician's office."

"I take my hat off to both of you. The medical field is tough and so very important to any society. I believe it really gives you a sense of service to your fellow citizens, especially being an ambulance driver, that's right out there on the front line. You actually get to save lives."

"Yes I have, but it can also be quite stressful."

"Yes it can, make sure to get in some good beach time where you can relax and recharge your batteries."

"I do like spending some time at the beach, but when we go on vacation we like to learn about the place where we are, so today was very interesting for us."

"So do you guys have any kids?" Ricky asked.

"No, not yet, but we're thinking about it." Carol replied.

"Are you religious?"

"Somewhat. We're both Episcopalian, but we don't let it rule our lives. We do believe in prayer and we go to church some-times, but we're not fanatical like some of our friends. Why? Do you have some advice for us?" she asked with a smile.

"Forgive me if I make you feel uncomfortable. I only asked because it's very important to be clear about your religion or lack of religion when you raise children. This is often an area where kids can get very confused, and the parents don't recognize it."

"We heard you were also some kind of preacher in the islands, is that true?"

"Well, I was raised as a Methodist, and when I was younger, I used to help out with Sunday School, but I have never been any kind of official minister or preacher."

"Oh, Methodist. That's very close to Episcopalians, isn't it."

"Yes," Ricky answered her, "I think all of the Christian denominations are very close to each other, in terms of their basic beliefs and philosophy."

"Even the Catholics?" Billy asked.

"Yes, even the Catholics. Of course you know they were the first one."

"Really, I thought Judaism was."

"What are you saying?" Billy piped in, "you know that's not a Christian denomination."

"Yeah, you're right, I think I'm getting confused because they both use the Old Testament."

"It's an easy mistake to make, that's why I brought up the topic in the first place," Ricky said.

"So, do you still teach Sunday School?" Carol enquired.

"No, I don't. A few years ago, I was doing a lot of thinking about the logistics of the Christian religion. I mean I've always been involved in it, and I just accepted the parts that were strange, because that's what I was taught, and I really never questioned it the way I do most other things. Anyway, the more I thought about it, the more I had to admit to myself, in all truthfulness and honesty, that it didn't make sense. It was based on myth and innuendo and people often in powerful positions interpreting illogical situations for you, that were based on some written material that had been translated from so many different languages, that it simply appeared unreasonable and so didactic. You have to do this and believe this, or something bad will happen to you. So I started to see it as a philosophy of fear."

"So do you believe in God?" Billy asked.

Ricky took a sip of his drink and looked out at the field beyond the parking lot and then out over the calm, blue water of the bay.

"Deep inside, I know how I feel whenever I'm asked that question, but it is always difficult to articulate and have the answer come out right. But I'll give it a shot. I don't believe in the God I was taught as a child. A powerful man-like figure with a white beard who created the universe and all the beings that live in it, and who chose a specific group to be his people, and who had a son that he had to crucify so that those who have the opportunity to learn about him, and only those, would go to some nirvana after death. I could go on, but I think you get the idea."

"I believe that there could be a higher power in the universe, but I just don't know. How many wonderful entities are simply natural or were they set in motion or created by some great power. I don't know. However, I do believe in the words and works of the man at the center of this religion. I do believe that Jesus of Nazareth existed. I do believe he was a wonderful prophet, and I often feel great love for him when I read about his teachings. His telling us to love one another, to be kind, to be humble, to always seek peace, to be willing always to turn the other cheek. These are the principles I try to follow. But I do not believe he was any more a son of a higher power than I am, I do not believe he was a savior, with all that comes with it. To me he was just an incredible prophet who tried to get his fellow Jews to practice what they supposedly believed. Does that make any sense?"

"Are you sure you're not a Harvard professor?" Carol asked.

"Just a taxi driver who thinks about things," he replied, smiling broadly.

"So, do you go to any kind of church now?" Billy asked.

"I'm glad you asked that," he said, still smiling. "About a year ago I thought about finding some kind of gathering place where people get together and discuss how they feel about life. I've always liked the concept of gathering together to discuss various life situations, maybe ponder their importance, especially the rules we feel are necessary to live by."

"So, in your searching, what did you find?"

"Well, if you don't mind my telling you, I will."

"Please go ahead," Billy said.

"It's a very different and interesting organization, for lack of a better term, I really don't see it as a church, but that's what it's called. It's the Unitarian Universalist Church. I sure wish I knew about it a long time ago, but I have to be grateful that I did find it. It has a group of members who believe in totally different religious philosophies, but they all get along."

"You mean like different denominations?"

"No, a lot more difference than that. Some are Christian, some Hindu, some Muslim, some atheists and others. It's like everyone is searching for their own truth, but they're accepting of the beliefs and philosophies that others have."

"Well, I must say that sounds very interesting. Of course I've heard of the Unitarian Church, and this other version, Unitarian Universal, but I always thought it was just another new Christian denomination. I know some of the founding fathers were Unitarian, but I was never really sure how close it was to other Christian denominations."

"As far as I know, some Unitarians do believe in God, but not in the idea of the trilogy. I believe in Jesus as a prophet who preached admirably about principles that the Jewish religion was built on, and were getting away from, but I don't believe they see him as God. Do you know what the Jeffersonian Bible is?"

"No," Billy answered.

"It's a version of the new Testament, written by Thomas Jefferson. What he basically did was write about Jesus' life as a man, and took out the miracles that the other New Testament writers had attributed to him."

"Why would Thomas Jefferson, a man who supposedly founded this country on Christian principles, do that?"

"I don't really know what was in Mr. Jefferson's head at the time, but for me it indicates that those guys were also searching for the truth, and didn't just accept what was taught to them without thinking about it. There were a number of Unitarians at the time, and I believe John Adams was one too. Anyway, I don't want to get caught up in the Unitarian religion, or sound like I'm proselytizing, but I am really comfortable and pleased with the Unitarian Universal version, which encompasses members with beliefs, far beyond Christianity. Anyway, what started this entire conversation, and sometimes I don't know when to shut up, is that I believe when parents teach their children about religion, they should be sure about it and the denomination they're teaching, so as not to confuse the kids."

"I think that's very good advice," Carol said, "we'll make sure we use it when the time comes."

"Well guys," Ricky said getting up and chuckling. "We've covered plantation slavery and religion. Any other casual topics you want to cover?" Before they could answer he continued. "Now we need to get back into the van for our trip to the ferry."

"Okay folks," Ricky said in a louder voice. "Finish your drinks and let's get back to our van for our return trip. Please tip your server, but you don't have to pay your bill, that's part of the tour."

107

The group piled into the van in the parking lot, as Wally said goodbye and wished them a pleasant rest of their visit. Ricky said a few words to him, shook hands warmly, and then opened the driver's door and made himself comfortable behind the steering wheel. He was soon driving out of the parking lot, on his way to the ferry dock in Cruz Bay. Jimmy was sitting next to Ricky in the passenger's seat, and Earl was sitting in the seat behind him.

Chapter Eight

C hapter 8

"That was a very interesting tour," Earl said, leaning and speaking quietly to Ricky. "I wasn't sure if it was a relaxing day at the beach and then an interesting tour of a historic event, or a serious lecture in how important it is for us to pay attention to the social ramifications of the terrible institution of slavery."

"I think it was both of those things," Jimmy said, leaning across to get closer to Earl and Ricky. "I knew we were going to be dealing with a serious historical event. Unfortunately slavery on a sugar plantation, by its very nature, is a lot more overwhelming than going to Shakespeare's birthplace or where Thoreau lived. This is more like going to a battlefield where many perished. What makes it different is that we have this horrible historic institution, on what has become a beautiful tropical island that people visit to relax and have fun. Talk about a contrast."

Ricky nodded his head back and forth, as he drove up on to the main road, but he didn't say anything. He wanted to hear what the two men had to say.

"In a way, it's really remarkable how ethnic differences in the U.S. always seem to be present. And so much of it comes from the institution of chattel slavery. I've been thinking a lot about it in the last couple of days, probably due to some conversations I've had with my good friend here, Mr. Ricky. Now, we have several areas of ethnic differences. Hispanics are different from Whites, so are Asians and Arabs, and don't start me on Native Americans, being from Oklahoma and all, but there's something about the way we enslaved Blacks and then made them second class citizens that was horrible. And so many of us when we think of Blacks back home, think of them as others, and we really don't realize it. And we pass these feelings on to our children, without realizing it."

"Yeah, you make a good point," Jimmy added, "but one thing I kept wondering about as I was walking around at Annaberg, was did the slaves there ever reach a point where they couldn't take it any more, and rebel against the owners?"

"That's an interesting thought. Did that ever happen Ricky?"

"There were a number of revolts on the plantations. Of course the owners tried to shut them down as quickly as possible so as to give the impression they were always in total control, but a lot of them left for fear of the violence and other hardships caused by the revolts."

Rick took a sip from his "roadie cup", cleared his throat, and spoke louder, so that everyone in the van could hear him.

"Guys, I have one more aspect of plantation life that I feel I should share with you, and it's based on the question Jimmy and Earl just asked; if there was ever a revolt by the slaves at the plantation. And the answer is yes, there was a revolt, quite a major one, but it wasn't just at Annaberg, it was most of the island, which had several other plantations."

"As you learned from Wally, slaves had to grow their own food in order to survive. In the seventeen thirties apparently there was a major hurricane and this was followed by a couple of years of drought on the island, and some of the slaves were literally starving to death. They responded by attempting to get food from the owners, who punished them severely for such actions."

"That's terrible. Why wouldn't they get food for them? How would they work?" Marjean said.

"Yes," Carol added, "that's even below being inhumane."

"Well," Ricky continued, "working was obviously very important, but so was having total control and dominance over the slaves and maintaining complete discipline. But when the enslaved people couldn't take it anymore, some felt they had nothing to lose, and they figured out a way to have a major rebellion. Apparently some of the slaves the Danes had recently brought from Africa, were from a warrior group instead of farmers who they tried to import, and the warrior group, known as Akwamus, devised a plot to smuggle homemade swords into

111

the fort in St. John, where the business of the island was carried out, and they fought and killed most of the Danes there, sent signals to the warriors at other plantations, and were therefore able to quickly take over most of the island. A lot of White Europeans whose plantations were close to the water, were able to escape to nearby islands by boat. A number of businessmen in St. Thomas owned plantations in St. John, which they hired overseers to run, and they put together a small force to try to take back St. John from the Akwamus, but the force was defeated."

"So, how long did the slaves control the island?" Marjean asked.

"They held it for about five months, until the Danes got the British to talk to the French, and they finally put together a force of about two hundred soldiers who came in from Martinique, and these trained warriors had enough fire power and training in war, to overcome the rebellion."

"What happened to the slaves?"

"Most of them were killed, Marjean. But tortured first, to send a message to the others. A number of them committed suicide to avoid the torture, or treatment when they went back to the plantation. But some of them also escaped to the other islands, and unfortunately these never left much of a record of their activities. So there you have a summary of the St. John slave rebellion of 1733."

"Thank you, Ricky," Jimmy said, "that's quite a story. I just had this feeling that there was some kind of rebellion here, as

I'm sure there were in many areas where there were plantations. I mean, how could there not be."

"I think you guys are beginning to understand," Ricky said.

No one replied to this remark, except Marjean who whispered to Ricky. "Yes we are."

As Ricky approached a fairly sharp left turn on the drive back, Jimmy gestured towards the windscreen that there were a couple of people at the side of the road.

"What do we have here?" Ricky said. "This couple seems lost. I'd better check this out and make sure they're okay."

There was a decent place to park that had very little grass on the opposite side of the road, so Ricky stopped the vehicle there, climbed out, crossed the road carefully, and walked up to the very pale complected couple, who looked as though they had arrived on the island that day.

"How you guys doing?" Ricky asked as he walked up to them.

"We're fine," the young man answered. He was wearing a large, white, Bob Marley t-shirt under his back pack, cut off jeans, and some well-worn navy sneakers. The young lady was in a yellow tank top with extremely short green shorts. "We're hikers, but I think we've missed our trail. We're trying to get down to Maho Bay, where we're going to spend a couple of days."

"Did you get here today?" Ricky asked.

"Yes, we were supposed to meet a couple of friends," the young woman replied, "but they had an emergency and had to leave St. Thomas, so we decided to come anyway and do some camping instead."

"Do you have reservations at Maho Bay?"

"No, the guy who dropped us to the ferry in St. Thomas, said we wouldn't have any trouble getting a tent," the young man said.

"By the way, I'm Ricky, a taxi driver, and I'm taking a bunch of people back to St. Thomas if you feel you want to go back there."

"I'm Larry, and this is Melody. Thanks, but we're okay, really. We want to do some camping."

"Okay, Larry and Melody, I'll walk you to where the path starts so that you can get down to Maho. It's not that far. I'll give you my card, and I want you to ask for Mickey when you get there and show him the card. If for some reason they're full, call my cell phone when you're with him. What about money, do you have enough?"

"We have our credit cards, but not much cash," he answered.

"Here," Ricky said, pulling out his wallet and extracting five twenties, "hang on to this in case of an emergency. It's always good to have some cash on you in these islands."

"You sure, how are we going to pay you back?"

"You have my number," Ricky said with a smile.

Ricky waved at the van and pointed, then he took the couple to the trail about fifty yards away. When he got there he shook hands with them.

"Once you get settled in guys, you'll be fine. And don't forget, ask for Mickey."

"Thank you, Ricky. We're very grateful. You guys are great on this island. And we will get this money back to you."

"Straight down and to the left past the big rock. Enjoy guys." He turned around and started making his way back to the van.

"Do you think he knew those people?" Carol asked.

"I don't think so," Marjean replied. "I think he stopped because he thought they might be in trouble. Lost or something."

"I'm pretty sure he didn't know them," Jimmy said. "Not only that, but I'm pretty sure I saw him give them or loan them some money."

"That's quite remarkable," Marjean said.

"That's my Mr. Ricky," Earl said, "a most unique and exceptional gentleman. I don't believe I ever really understood what enlightenment and logic meant until I met him. And he does it so easily. He just talks to you about normal, everyday things, and suddenly you're questioning them and asking why would supposedly intelligent people do something or believe in something that's taken for granted, but really ridiculous when you examine it."

"What everyday things are you referring to?" Jimmy asked.

"Things like racism, the way we feel about people of different ethnicities. Religion would be another one. Stuff that we say and even believe, but don't make sense when you really examine them. Sexism; especially the way men treat women and dictate how they should act, how they should behave."

"It sounds like your friend Mr. Ricky is a very astute sociologist, especially as it applies to the rules of life that we often follow without asking why," Luke spoke slowly.

"He's a very intelligent man," Marjean added, "very smart."

"You guys really think Ricky is that special?" Jimmy asked. "I mean he gave us a very good tour of the slave plantation, and that young man he hired was excellent. He put together a good tour for tourists, I'll give you that, but that's his job, and it's not that hard to get some information from history, and study up on it. But he's just a taxi driver for Christ's sake, not Albert Einstein."

"As my husband said after a conversation with Mr. Ricky. He'll make you think whether you want to or not. And I submit to you, that's exactly what we're doing right now," Marjean said. Then she turned to look at Earl, who gave her the thumbs up sign. There were a few heads in the van, nodding in agreement.

A few minutes later, they heard feet scuffling in the high grass on the other side of the road as Ricky got ready to cross over to the dirt area where the van was parked. He arrived at the van, pulled the door open and looked at everyone.

"My apologies, folks. Sorry I had to take off like that, not very professional of me, but that young couple looked rather out of place over there, and I didn't want to risk leaving them to get into trouble. I told them who to talk to at the Maho camp grounds, and showed them the short cut to get there, so they should be fine."

He climbed into the van, put on his seat belt, started up the engine, and added, "We should still get to Cruz Bay in time to catch the 5 o'clock ferry. Now sit back and enjoy the ride into town. It's still too early for the full sunset, but if you look out over the shoreline and the islands to your right, you can see the afternoon sun starting to go down, which I've always found quite pretty."

"So, you really didn't know those people?" Jimmy said.

"No, I didn't, but when you've driven around here as much as I have, you get a sense for when people are lost or confused, especially visitors who really don't know the place and can get lost."

"And it looked as though you actually gave them some money," Jimmy continued.

"Yes, I loaned them some cash in case they had to go to a shop or some other business that doesn't take credit cards. There are still some like that in the V.I."

"And you think they're going to repay you?"

"Yes, I do. I gave them my card, and I have a credit card account. All they have to do is give me the number."

"I think you're rather naive," Jimmy continued, "but I'm glad you have that kind of belief in people doing the right thing. Unfortunately where I grew up I would expect them to rip me off."

"Sometimes I do too, but I'd rather lose some money than read about something bad that happened to them in tomorrow's newspapers."

117

"Do you see yourself as some kind of ambassador for the islands?" Carol asked.

"Yes I do. I think everyone who is employed in the tourist industry should feel they're an ambassador for the island they represent. I try to relate this concept to all of my fellow workers in the industry. But it works both ways. If we expect you guys to enjoy your stay and want to return, then we have to be sincere and believe in what we do, and be competent and efficient. But not only as it relates to tourism, but to how we feel about life in general. I think we should all know who we are, what we believe and why we believe it. And always be willing to help each other when circumstances warrant it."

"Okay, you're on. I'll let you know."

Chapter Nine

Chapter 9

R icky pulled the borrowed van into the parking lot at a quarter to five. He parked and walked around helping everyone in the group out of the vehicle, making sure to remind everyone to take their belongings with them. He then locked the van and took the group past the ticket booth, where he left the keys with the attendant.

The ferry left the dock in even calmer water than earlier. Jimmy's wife, Kathy, sat next to Ricky, and they both looked to the west as the sun seemed to be descending faster because of the mid-winter time zone. The golden shards from the orb were giving way to some pink cotton over the clear turquoise sea. She leaned over close to Ricky, and said in a hoarse, whispery voice, "that's beautiful."

"Yes, it is. It should be a lot pinker by the time we get to St. Thomas."

"Today was very special. We all really had a good time, and also learned a lot."

"Thank you," Ricky said. "I try to maintain the interest every time I take a group to Annaberg. Today was a very good bunch. Interesting people who were fully engaged in the subject matter. Can't ask for more than that."

"Tell me, is it very difficult for people on the Mainland to move to St. Thomas to live?"

Ricky was surprised by this question and looked closely at Katherine for a long two minutes. "You sure don't beat around the bush," he said.

"I'm sorry, didn't mean to be so forward, but I don't know when I'll get a chance to talk to you like this again; besides I'm sure you've been asked this a number of times, and obviously have a lot of experience answering it."

"Yes, I have heard this question a barrel-full of times over the years. Let me ask you this? Did you guys start thinking about this since you've been here, or have you spent some time looking into it when you were at home?"

"Actually we've been talking about the possibility of living in the islands for a while, maybe a year or so. At first it was Hawaii and other Pacific areas, but we think we would like being in this part of the world better."

"Well, the first area you want to look at is the economics of moving. It's important that you can live comfortably while you're getting used to a new place, especially one with a vastly different culture than you're used to. This is especially true if you have children. It's hard enough getting used to St. Thomas if you have the means to be comfortable. It's almost It's almost impossible if you have to struggle to make ends meet financially while you're figuring it out, and you have to keep in mind that a small island with a relatively small population has a higher cost of living than almost anywhere on the Mainland."

"We don't have kids, and once we make the decision to move and we liquidate some of our assets in New York, we'd probably be quite comfortable financially. We own a fairly successful restaurant just outside Queens, and we can either sell it or have someone run it for us to provide us with the income we'll need."

"If you have a good business and someone you trust to run it for you and maintain the profits, it would probably be best to hang on to it, in case you didn't like where you moved to, and decided to return. There are also a number of residents here who spend about half the year or so in either place, so there are options."

"What would you say the most difficult thing to get used to is, if you moved from the Mainland to here?"

"For almost all Statesiders, the single biggest difference is living in a community, not only where the majority of people are black, but where Blacks also control the government and administration of the islands. Our governor is usually black, as are most of our senators and other government officials. A number of the wealthiest and most influential people on the islands are also black. And no matter how you twist or turn it, if you've never lived in a community like this, it takes getting used to."

"Okay, we've actually given this area a lot of thought, but as you said, it will still take getting used to. So, what else?"

"We're also a rather liberal community in other social areas."

"What do you mean?"

"We also have a fairly large gay community in St. Thomas."

"I think it's safe to say we have one in New York too"

"Yes you do, but it is not as open or acceptable as the one here. In fact, a number of my Gay friends are from New York, and they've moved because they are much more accepted here for who they are. Anyway, I thought I should let you know, because I do know a number of couples who were very uncomfortable when same-sex couples were being intimate in front of them, especially the men."

"I see what you're saying, but why would they think like this. It's none of their business."

"If we've been conditioned when we were very young to believe that homosexuality is wrong, or distasteful, or unnatural, or perhaps UnChristian or even sinful, then it's difficult to throw off that coat of conditioning or even brainwashing when we become adults. Many of us will have these beliefs from our early years and maintain them throughout our lives. I personally believe this is why we have so many problems in society. Unless we become a part of some program, whether it's college or some other group, we will never change our various prejudices, whether they be homophobia, or racism or sexism, or anything else."

"You know, you're probably right. I've never thought about it like that, and you just throw it out there as if you're talking about the weather."

"Well, I think about this stuff a lot, so it's pretty easy and quite natural to throw it out there, as you said." Ricky smiled innocently as he said this as if to indicate this was just a light, innocent conversation about the V.I. Kathy was smiling too, but she was well aware of the depth of the conversation.

"So what else should we know about S.Thomas?"

"Our medical care is not the best."

"Do you have poorly trained doctors or bad hospitals?"

"Our hospital is quite good, and we have some very good physicians. The problem is that we don't have enough specialists. So we'll have an excellent orthopedic doctor to diagnose your problem, and an excellent surgeon to fix it, but at the same time our gastro guy had to leave and we haven't been able to replace him for several months. Now you can find a good doctor in that field in Puerto Rico, but it's inconvenient to go there, especially if you have to see the doctor several times."

"What about emergency service?"

"Our ambulances are quite reliable and efficient, but it's also wise to have an air ambulance insurance policy, especially if you think you might have a more serious preexisting condition. This is a company that would fly you off island for major treatment, usually some form of emergency surgery."

"So, you have to consider all of this to live in the American Paradise?"

"I think it's always good to understand as much as you can about a new place when you're considering moving there. Better to know possibilities than to be totally surprised."

"Yes, you're right of course, and I do appreciate the info. And you haven't said anything about hurricanes yet."

"No, I haven't, but there are storms all over the world, and we all have to deal with them as best we can. The one good thing about hurricanes, if there is such a thing, is that you usually have a day or two warning to decide if you want to endure them or leave the island; depending of course on your ability to endure."

"And presumably there are some positive aspects to living here too," she said, smiling.

"I thought I'd leave the good stuff for the last. So here is my opinion of my Caribbean/American island home."

"Even though there's a strong, pervading Caribbean culture present," Ricky said slowly. "No one ever forgets we are a part of the United States. We have a very positive mix of Black locals, Blacks who have emigrated from other islands, Whites from the Mainland , Blacks from the Mainland, Puerto Ricans who identify as Hispanic and a small but growing group of people from India."

"In St.Thomas we tend to know each other quite well, but we don't intrude on the private lives of others. However, if someone we know needs help or gets into trouble, we do help out. In the business and professional community, people are not that interested in appearing successful or prominent. I mean there are a few, especially those who haven't been on the island very long, but for the most part we're more interested in doing a good job. And when I talk about the business community, I'm including the small businessman as well. So if you go to a bar for a drink after work in the afternoon, you'll see small businessmen like myself, or fishermen, or carpenters and local government workers deep in conversation about various subjects.

"Sounds very interesting, like one giant bar scene," she said.

"In a way it is, but besides having fun and unwinding from the hard work required when you live on a beautiful tourist island, we do get some serious events planned. Things like fund raising dinners for those in need, supporting sports events for kids, and also organizing sports for ourselves."

"And I imagine you guys also discuss some of that social stuff when you're around."

"I have to plead guilty. I bring it up most of the time, as I truly believe that if we learn to think for ourselves, and not only in the way we were conditioned to think as kids, people who we've been taught to see as inferior, would be treated better and we would all have a more positive life experience. I'll just say one more thing on this topic. I believe the word we should use more is 'why?' Why is our religion better than others? Why do we need to have a religion? Why are some ethnic groups considered better than others? Why can't we mix freely with other ethnicities? Why do men treat women as inferior? Why do women feel they have to behave a certain manner to be accepted by men? Why do we think we have to appear successful to others? I could go on, but I think you get the point. In short, why do we accept so many illogical and hurtful rules for life? Why don't we stand up to society and seriously question them?"

"You're a very interesting gentleman, Mr. Ricky. I get the feeling you say these things to most people you meet."

"I do, Katherine, just about everyone I meet. As John Lennon said in his great song, 'Imagine' - You may believe I'm a dreamer but I'm not the only one. I hope someday you'll join us and the world will live as one."

"But how can society work if we don't have rules to follow? We have to have some idea of what's right and what isn't "

"Yes, you're right, we do need rules to follow. But who gets to make up the rules? And who gives them the right to make the rules?"

"But haven't some of the rules been around a long time? Ah, let me think. Honor thy father and thy mother for example."

"If your father is a good, by all means, honor him. If he's kind and loving and helps those around him and is humble and not prideful and does his best to provide for you and teaches you to be a strong individual and to care equally for all people, regardless of race, then by all means honor him. But if your father steals, and mistreats his family and hates people because they are of different ethnicities, then what is there to honor? He should have to earn that honor, not just get it because he's your father. But going back to who makes the rules, if we take a close look at history, we find that those who make up the rules are those who benefited most from them. So a proven formula used by people in power, was to make up the rules that suited them, particularly economically, and then find something in religion to justify it. This was done many, many times, and even today this formula is still utilized. I don't know if you realize it, but you pulled out a religious justification from the Old Testament when you said honor thy father and thy mother."

"We were at a former slave plantation today," Ricky continued. "Who gave these people the right to capture and own other people and say it's okay because they had support from so-called religious teachers who interpreted some passage in some book that said some deity, who supposedly represented good, said it was okay. How could this atrocity last over two hundred years? And how could over a hundred thousand men, if not more, claiming to be civilized, give their lives in an attempt to keep this horrendous practice? Basically, the majority of people in this country accepted the rules that those who profited made up, and no matter how hard they tried to justify it, they all knew it was wrong. And it took over two centuries before finally there were enough citizens who were finally willing to to make the ultimate sacrifice in order to end the institution of chattel slavery."

"I understand what you're saying, and I do appreciate your passion. You're right, we all tend to take many aspects of life for granted, instead of asking some questions, and also making the effort to get some answers. As a woman, there certainly have been a number of times in my life when I found myself being pushed into a corner and instead of fighting back, I accepted being suppressed or pushed around, because that's what I thought society expected from me as a woman."

"You hit the nail on the head, Katherine. This is exactly what I'm talking about. And to put it bluntly, if you accept being treated as inferior to men, it will never change. It is so important that you know your worth, your value, and assert yourself."

"Thank you, Mr. Ricky, thank you for your wise words."

The ferry slowed down drastically and started pulling into the dock at Red Hook. The sun sinking into the sea to the west had truly designed a beautiful, pink, photographic sunset.

"Well, here we are, back on St. Thomas, or back on the rock as we locals would say." Ricky stood up and spoke to the group. "Time to disembark, folks, and don't forget your personal stuff."

Fifteen minutes later Ricky was pulling out of the parking area and turning right, on to the Red Hook road. This time Jimmy was sitting next to him in the front seat.

"I hope you don't mind Kathy asking you about the various nuances of living on St. Thomas. She said you had a really good conversation about it."

"No, I don't mind at all. It's hard to appreciate how the island works unless you've lived here for a while, but I like to give people considering residency at least some general ideas on what to expect."

"We certainly appreciate the advice. But there's one area I haven't heard much about and that's the politics of the V.I. I know a lot of people don't like to talk about politics for fear of having a disagreeable discussion with who they're talking to, but that doesn't bother me, and I would really be interested in knowing what the politics are like here. That is if you don't mind talking about it."

"Not at all," Ricky said," I could talk about politics all day, and even all night, if needed." He smiled at this statement and then added, "I believe we should not only talk about politics, but really get to understand how it works in the community, especially a small one like this one."

"So would you say that most voters in the V.I are Democrats?"

"Yes, most of us are registered Democrats, but we have a decent representation in the Republican Party, and even the Independent Party."

"I would have thought with all the small, independent businesses you have here you'd have more Republicans."

"Many of the business owners I know are progressive politically. I really don't see why you'd want to be a Republican just because you're in business."

"Well, I'm sure you know the old saying, Republicans are for business. Democrats are for taxes," Jimmy said with a haughty laugh.

"So are you saying that Republicans don't believe in taxes?"

"I guess if you have to pay them you do, but who wants to pay taxes?"

"So without taxes how do you pay for schools, or the police department, or firemen or medical care when you're older and can't work?"

"I'm not against the government taking out some taxes for necessary services, but I think they take out a lot more than they need, and end up wasting a lot of our hard earned money."

"But do you know for a fact where this wasted money goes, or are you just repeating vague political phrases that are used by conservatives to gain some kind of political advantage over progressives. Let me ask you this, who do you think you pay most of your taxes to, local government or the federal government?"

"If you include sales tax, gas tax and property taxes along with the other smaller taxes, I think I actually pay more locally."

" I'm in no way a tax expert," Ricky said with a laugh, "but I believe most of us do pay more to our local governments. Those of us who are extremely wealthy and pay our fair share, will pay more to the federal government. And the reason I bring this up, is because many Americans who complain about paying too much in taxes, think it all goes to the federal government."

"Yes, I agree with you there, many people don't realize they pay more in local taxes. But don't you think there's a lot more waste when Democrats are in power?"

"In general, I believe most of the federal budget goes to Social Security, Medicare, other healthcare benefits, education and of course the military. I believe these are all important in any society. Also, when Republicans are in power I don't notice any decrease in my taxes."

"That's another good point. I really don't either, but I hear Republican politicians say that all the time. Now, I'm an independent, as I feel I should look at both sides and decide which has the better solution on any given issue. Being a business owner though, I do tend to lean a little more right."

"Once again, I don't think you have any logical reason to say that, except it's a myth you've heard many times and taken for granted without any real proof that it has merit." I'm a businessman too, and I see no reason whatsoever to lean or even tilt slightly to the right politically. You're probably going to say next, that we have too much regulation and it hurts business." Ricky chuckled when he said this.

"Well, now that you mention it, wouldn't you like to get rid of some or even most of the regulations that business people have to adhere to?"

"Actually, I think some more regulation, or laws, which is what they really are, should be added, especially where the processed food industry is concerned. I believe a lot of additives are put in processed food and it's harmful to the public."

"Don't you believe people should have the freedom to eat and drink whatever they choose, good or bad?"

"It's not really freedom if they don't know what's in it."

"So, if the government has proof that the additives are harmful, why is it allowed in the first place?"

"This is where our practice of lobbying comes into play."

"Lobbyists? What do they have to do with it? Aren't they mainly concerned with basic laws?"

"These are laws," Ricky said. "Here's an example. Some members of Congress are presented with the results of testing on sodas, and are informed that a regular can of soda has ten teaspoons of sugar in it. They decide to pass a law that says the soda industry can't put more than five teaspoons in the can, due to its strong connection to diabetes. The soda companies are concerned they will lose profits if this happens, so they send their highly paid lobbyists to some of the more vulnerable congressmen, and they do whatever it takes to get them to vote against changing the law, and maintain the ten teaspoons of sugar in the soda, which maintains the profits for the companies. So, the businesses continue to make a lot of money, and the citizens continue to get sick. This is the problem I have with the kind of conservative thinking that says big profits are good for everyone and somehow represent freedom."

"You do have a point, and I must say you've obviously done your homework, but don't you think Republicans have done some good things for our citizens? For example, returning to slavery, and the fact that the majority of the people in the V.I. are black; don't they feel they owe the Republicans a lot, seeing they were the party to end slavery, under Lincoln?"

"The first thing to bear in mind when we discuss the end of slavery as I mentioned earlier, is that other countries, like England for example, had already ended the institution over thirty years before, so the U.S. government was under some severe pressure to end it as well. The political parties in the eighteen sixties were nothing like they became in the nineteen sixties when President Johnson signed the civil rights and voting rights acts. This is the date that the Democratic Party became progressive, or liberal. Before the nineteen sixties the Democratic Party was far more conservative than the Republicans, especially in the South."

"You think the Democrats were conservative?" Jimmy asked.

"They certainly were. They were the main party in the South during the Civil War. It was the party of White Supremacy and apartheid. Southern Democrats were also in favor of the Jim Crow laws after the war, that led to the terrible dehumanization and suppression of Black people. For example, the members of the greatest white supremacy group, the Ku Klux Klan, were all Democrats. There were also other political parties in our history; the Whig party, and in Lincoln's time there was the Democratic Republican Party. But I think the best way to simplify all of this is to think of our parties and leaders in terms of Liberal and Conservative. Up until President Johnson's term, I believe the country, including the main political parties was basically conservative, as the majority of countries were. It's just that some leaders were more conservative than others. So even though most of the laws in the country pertaining to social values were conservative, the act of ending slavery was liberal. However, not allowing Blacks to eat at certain restaurants or stay in certain hotels or drink at certain water fountains etc., was very conservative. This is basically what the Civil Rights Act ended in 1964."

"Are you serious?" Jimmy asked loudly. This is why most Virgin Islanders are Democrats? They know all this stuff? Man, I feel like I'm at a college lecture."

Ricky could hear Earl chuckling in the seat behind him, he was obviously listening to the conversation, but didn't say anything.

"When you are affected by various adversities in life, you tend to pay more attention to them in school."

"I suppose you're right," Jimmy agreed.

"But it's not just because Liberals are more sensitive to the way blacks have been treated, there are other minorities in the V.I. too. As I told your wife when she asked me about what it's like living here, we have a lot of what I call social minorities, like Gay people who are often discriminated against on the Mainland. We also have a sort of identity formed out of island life, that does not care for the traditional mores and conservative rules of society as a whole. We are also a very knowledgeable political population. This is helped by the size of the island, but we tend to be very aware not only of the local politics, but also what goes on politically nationally. When cable t.v. came in it made it much easier, but now with the internet it's even more prominent."

"And this is why you're a Demo....Ah, I mean liberal?"

"Yes, a few of the reasons."

"You mean there are more?"

"Oh yes, I haven't gotten into expanded health care or abortion rights or better gun control, but these are some other reasons why I feel the way I do."

"Well, I think about several of these issues or listen to lawmakers talk about them, and I believe most of them have two sides to them, which is why I like to think it through from an independent standpoint before coming to a decision on how I really feel about the solution to these problems."

"You know Jimmy, when I was younger and just starting to vote, I was also an independent, because somehow it made me feel like I had a more open mind about issues, instead of prejudging them. Then one day my wife sat with me at the dinner table and asked me to go through every political issue I could think of, and tell her which ones I would vote on from a conservative point of view."

"And were you honest in your response?"

"Yes, very honest. I couldn't find one. So, my friend, I'll ask you to do the same thing. Think through all the issues you can think of, and be specific and more importantly logical in your response to them, and tell me in a couple of days how right leaning independent you really think you are."

"Okay, you're on. I'll let you know."

Chapter Ten

C hapter 10

Ricky could hear Earl chuckling a bit louder as he turned the van right, into the Sapphire Beach Resort driveway. He drove all the way to the front of the resort where the lobby was, then got out of the van and helped some of the group with their bags and walked into the lobby with them. They all thanked him for the most intriguing outing, and said that they hoped to see him again. Ricky told them that he could put together a trip to a private beach on St. Thomas on Wednesday, and he would leave a sign-up sheet at the front desk.

As he was putting the sheet together to leave with the assistant manager, Earl and Marjean walked up to him. Earl placed a hand on his shoulder, and spoke.

"My good friend, Mr. Ricky, you never cease to amaze me. That was an incredible trip today. I don't know where you find the energy. I hope you have the energy to have a cold one at the bar with us before you leave. You can think of it as your unwinding drink."

"It would be nice if you could join us," Marjean added.

"I have some time before I have to leave," Ricky said. "Let me go and park the van, I'll be right back."

Ricky was soon back at the bar, sitting between Earl and Marjean. Barry was still tending bar, and asked Ricky what he wanted.

"A light beer would be fine thanks; something to quench the thirst."

"If this is one of your typical Monday visits to Annaberg I imagine you have built up quite a thirst. You've probably been lecturing on plantation life and related subjects most of the day." He put the light beer down in front of Ricky and made a small bow.

"Sounds like you know your friend quite well, Mr. Barry," Earl said. "He increased our knowledge and understanding about a subject so many of us want to ignore, by a considerable amount today."

"I hope you guys realize that you were probably treated to something very special. I've never heard anyone explain a subject as well as Ricky."

"Oh, we appreciate it very much," Marjean added. "He also had a very knowledgeable young man, Wally, who gave us some great information about the plantation. He was very thorough and made it really interesting for us."

Barry saw a couple get into seats across the bar, and went over to take an order from them.

"You really talked a lot today, Mr Ricky. Besides the stuff related to the tour, you really were involved in a lot of conversations. Jimmy and his wife, that other couple, Carol and Billy," Marjean said.

"And don't forget the couple on the road who were lost," Earl reminded them.

Ricky took a long drink and leaned back in his chair. "Yes, I guess I really did a lot of talking today. But sometimes I feel I owe it to people to answer their questions when I can."

"That was a lot more than just answering questions," Earl said, "especially with Jimmy."

"Ah, Jimmy and Katherine. Interesting couple. Really enjoyed chatting with them. You know, they were asking me about what it was like living here, and they were quite serious. I believe they've been thinking of the possibility of moving from the big city to somewhere a little different, like one of the islands."

"Really, I was doing some eavesdropping but didn't get that part. Maybe we should think about that too, honey," he said to Marjean. They both laughed at the remark, then became a little more serious. "You never know. It might be feasible in a few years," Earl said.

"So if we go to this private beach on Wednesday, where would we go?" Marjean asked Ricky.

"I have a friend whose family owns some land over on the north side, and at the edge of the land is a beach. It's a bit difficult to get to, and during the week it's often quite isolated. I just thought it would be nice to go there with a picnic basket and a couple of coolers, and have a nice quiet relaxing day. I feel like I know you guys really well, even though we just met, as I do about most of the group we had on the tour today. In my business sometimes you meet a group of people that you just get along well with. And this group is one of those."

"You know, when I was talking with you earlier today," Marjean said slowly, "we talked about various behaviors we learned from our parents and other adults when we were very young. And I kind of feel that underneath all the historical material about how terrible slavery was, and how Gay people who live on the island are more comfortable, and how liberal most of the people who live here are, as I heard you telling Jimmy, I start to see a theme to what you're really getting at."

"What do you think I'm getting at?" Ricky said with an impish grin.

"I think you're really questioning how we believe various things, like behaviors," she said almost in a whisper.

"I think you're catching on. Don't worry, I'll tell you all about it before you leave."

"Tell you all about what?" Earl asked.

"You'll find out," Rick answered with a smile.

"Excuse me guys, I've got to go to the bathroom. Be right back." Ricky pushed his chair back and walked away from the bar towards the bathrooms.

Barry walked over to Earl, whose glass was empty, and asked him if he wanted a refill. Earl nodded his assent, and Barry leaned over to pick up a bottle of dark rum.

"Can I ask you a question about Mr. Ricky?" Marjean asked the bartender.

"You've known him a long time, haven't you?"

"Yes, since we were boys," he said as he put Earl's drink in front of him. "We played soccer together on our high school team. He had quite a strong left foot, and was pretty fast."

"I wouldn't have taken him for much of an athlete."

"Oh, Ricky was pretty good."

"He does a lot more than just driving a taxi and taking people on tours, doesn't he?"

"Many of us do different types of jobs on the island. We don't feel we have to have one identity as people do on the Mainland. For example, I also do some bookkeeping, mostly helping people with their tax returns."

"Well, that sounds interesting. What else does Mr. Ricky do?"

"You know, he doesn't tell me everything, but from some of our conversations I think he does some consulting work with one of the government departments. He's fairly well known on the island, and his opinion is sometimes sought after by government officials, depending on what area they need some advice. As you've probably noticed, he's a very interesting man with some very interesting ideas about life."

"Barry, you wouldn't be putting me on?" she said with a laugh.

"I'm sure Ricky will explain everything to you guys when he's ready. Now let me get you a fresh drink."

When Ricky got back to the bar, the two other couples in his group, Jimmy and Katherine, and Billy and Carol, were also there. They had apparently showered and changed, and were involved in a fairly animated conversation when Ricky sat down. He heard the words "thought-provoking" being mentioned several times as he sat down in front of Barry.

"I think some of these guys are beginning to catch on to your little organization. Marjean was asking if I knew what you really did."

"Yeah, I figured she'd be the first to catch on. I plan to give them the whole scoop on Wednesday when we go to Browning beach."

"Wish I could be there, but Sapphire needs me."

"Jimmy was just telling us about the little assignment you gave him about being an Independent in our political system," Earl said. "Then Billy said he was an independent too, and he would give some serious thought to doing the same thing."

"Uh, oh. Here we go again," Barry said smiling broadly. "More politics."

Billy leaned over when he heard his name being mentioned, and gave a little wave to Ricky in order to be recognized. "So, Jimmy also told me most of the residents on the island were Democrats, including yourself, and I just wanted to hear why you are."

The group all pulled their chairs closer, around Ricky so they could hear him.

"You guys sure you want to hear about this now, after all the social and historical material I talked about today. I would have thought you're pretty tired of listening to me by now, after all, you're on vacation."

"We like to hear your opinion," Carol said. "You have a clear and simple way of talking about things that can be complicated."

"Basically I just tell you what I feel, and also why I feel a certain way."

"So tell us why you're a Democrat, or a liberal," Jimmy said.

"Well, my friend, seeing you said liberal, I'll follow that line of thought and tell you why I'm not a conservative. First I should tell you why I asked Jimmy to examine his political affiliation as an Independent. It was because I also used to think of myself as an Independent, of course this was a long time ago," he added with a grin. "Anyway, I used to think there were two reasonable sides to a situation, and after examining them I'd be able to identify the right one."

"I always thought you might be an Independent," Luke said with a laugh as he pulled up a chair and joined the rest of the group. "Sorry to interrupt, Mr Ricky, please continue."

"Well as I was saying, I used to be an Independent before my wife, Annette, asked me to examine my political philosophy and see if I could find anything in it that could be even remotely conservative, or that would merit looking at some political other side. So I did. I tried to take conservatism down to its lowest common denominator and define exactly what I thought it was."

"Where did you start?" Billy asked, "with the founding fathers?"

"No, I started well before the founding fathers. I could have started a thousand years before the founding fathers, because with the exception of one or two failed attempts like Athens or maybe Rome, the entire world was completely conservative. So I picked the period when the colonization of the new world began, the late fifteenth and early sixteenth centuries and took a look at all the western governments. Practically all of them were run by monarchies, which meant that the leadership was handed down without merit, and was totally authoritarian. The leaders were all exceptionally wealthy and powerful, and did everything possible to maintain the status of their subjects' lives, most of whom lived in poverty and ignorance. In other words they didn't want anything to change. They wanted to conserve this way of life, to hold on to it, in order to hold on to their own power. And besides a strong army, they did everything possible to prevent the peasants from becoming educated. They were deathly afraid of what would happen if the proletariat could read and write. But people did know how to read and write, mostly the aristocrats and the clergy, and even though it took another two hundred years, eventually enough people in a population began to believe that some god really didn't give these rulers the divine right to rule. However, some citizens started to look at these ultra conservative ways of life, which consisted mainly of the wealthy owning the land and the illiterate peasants working the land for very little, and they realized they could break down some of these social barriers and make life more tenable for more people. I would say this all started right around the beginning of the eighteenth century, and slavery was one of the first conservative practices that liberals in the west wanted to get rid of."

"I also happen to believe that most of our founding fathers were putting forward a liberal philosophy when they came up with the Constitution."

"You believe that the U.S. Constitution is a liberal philosophy," Billy said. "I always thought it was the opposite."

"That's what Conservatives want you to believe. You hear meaningless statements like Conservatives are for freedom and Liberals are for government."

"And you don't think that's true?" Billy continued.

"No, because it's all government. When Conservatives are in power there is no less government. The only thing that changes is where our taxes go. For example, Conservatives will spend money on the armed forces or on oil discovery. Liberals will spend money on health care or protecting the environment. But let's go back to some of the social issues that were evident as our politics began to become more sophisticated and better understood by our population. So we know about the social dehumanization of slavery. A large part of our country, a number of Southern states wanted to secede and form their own country in order to keep the institution. Many of the males were willing to fight and die for this, and over a quarter of a million did, some historians believe as many as half a million. And remember the war was fought about thirty years after England had ended slavery in their colonies, so the institution was already coming to an end."

"I didn't realize England had ended slavery that long before us. I always thought it was around the same time," Jimmy said.

"You know when the best time to end slavery was?" Ricky asked the group.

"You're asking us?" Billy said.

"Yes, when do you think?"

Luke cleared his throat and spoke in a serious tone. "The best time would have been during President George Washington's term, shortly after the Constitution was ratified."

"That's right. We wrote the constitution for a country based on the notion that all men were created equal and had rights. Wouldn't it have been great if they simply said slavery was wrong and they were going to end it. We would have been the first to do this. This would have made us look like we believed in what we said."

"I can't argue with that," Jimmy said. "But what makes you think it was the Conservatives who didn't want to end slavery?"

"Because this is what conservatism means. It means to keep the way of life the same. To maintain the system. To not change. To conserve."

"I can't argue with that," Luke said.

"Another social inequity that existed throughout history, but was coming to a head in the late nineteenth century in our country, was Women's Rights. Basically, what was a woman's place in society? The conservative position was that a woman's job in life was to be subservient to her husband, basically to serve him. She couldn't vote in elections or hold positions in government, unless she was born into a royal family of course, or receive any form of higher education. Liberals wanted to liberate women, to put them on an equal, or at least a more equal footing with their husbands. This led to the struggle for women to achieve the vote, which they did with the signing of the nineteenth amendment in nineteen twenty. Of course at that time it was mainly White women, but it was a big change. So, if I was an Independent weighing the pros and cons of that situation, I would definitely have agreed with the Liberals."

"Then after slavery and a few decent years of reconstruction, racism, particularly in the South, grew at a monumental rate under a system known as Jim Crow. Once again, the conservative position was alienating American citizens from the rights that Thomas Jefferson said they had. Laws were passed to prevent Black people from drinking at the same water fountains as Whites, or eating in the same restaurants or sleeping in the same hotels. And the Supreme Court upheld a law, Plessy versus Ferguson, that Louisiana could make it legal to have Blacks ride in different train cars than whites. This actually made segregation legal, nationally, which of course was the conservative position that they wanted to maintain, forever. So, once again I would have sided with the liberal position, which said segregation was immoral and should have been illegal."

"Conservatives have never been in favor of public education. The greatest threat to conservation is for people to be well educated. This is because well educated citizens can see how ridiculous many of the rules they want us to live by are."

"What are some of the rules?" Billy's wife, Carol asked.

"Rules like Whites are smarter and more important than Blacks. Men are better than women. Being gay is unnatural, and in the Bible it says that this is a sin. We should adhere to the Christian religion, even though it is illogical and has been used to control people for centuries. These rules extend into many of our life decisions. Who to marry, what job to have, how to dress. Many of us are taught these irrational rules as children and unfortunately if we don't question and change them as we get older, we're condemned to adhere to them for the rest of our lives. These are all conservative, so again I would come down on the side of the liberals, who work to change these rules. I can get into these even more, but let me hold off for now."

"Whenever you say that, you end up explaining social values even more," Earl said with a laugh. Marjean laughed and nodded her head as well.

"What can I say, I guess I don't know when to shut up." Ricky also laughed at himself.

Barry put a light beer in front of him. "Here," he said, "I think you need this."

"Ah, that's good," Ricky said after taking a long gulp. "Now, let me get back to my final point. In general, I believe the leaders of all the countries throughout history, and also the leaders of society, were extremely powerful and wealthy people, who used extremely influential, conservative principles to maintain the status quo, in order to retain their power. The entire world was conservative, including our country, and little by little what little liberal thinking there was, chipped away at it, until through the force of education those liberal voices chipped away enough to make some substantial changes in society."

"But going back to politics, a major occurrence took place in nineteen sixty-four. The civil rights movement was beginning to get quite prominent. Martin Luther King was speaking constantly on the plight of Black people, and much of America was listening. The great March on Washington was in August nineteen sixty-three and unfortunately President Kennedy was assassinated three months later. This made Lyndon Johnson President, and even though he was a Southern Democrat, who were extremely conservative, he signed what was arguably the most liberal legislation ever. The civil rights act in 1964, followed by the voting rights act a year later, probably brought Blacks closer to equality with Whites than anything else in our history. However there were serious ramifications of these bills. The Democratic Party at the time was a strange combination of extreme conservatism in the South, and more centrist in the Northeast, and the West. So when Lyndon Johnson signed those two liberal civil rights bills, he actually said the Democrats would probably lose the South forever, and sure enough practically all of the Southern States became Republican. This was the big switch in American politics, and it's why I like to deal with liberal and conservative instead of Democrats and Republicans. Unfortunately as time has gone on, a lot of citizens, especially younger ones, believe that we always had two political parties, and their philosophies have never changed."

"That's my last speech for tonight. I promise," he said with that large grin.

"You sure about that?" Earl said. "Sometimes I think you can go on forever."

"I think Mr. Ricky has said a lot to us today, starting with me at breakfast this morning. He has certainly given us a lot of historical information on human interaction in society and I for one am very grateful, but as much as I would like him to stay and maybe have dinner with us, I believe he's had a long day and should go home soon and get some rest."

Ricky quickly finished his beer, got up from the bar, said goodbye to the group, reminded them of the trip to Browning Beach, winked at Barry, and walked out to his van in the parking lot.

The group sat at the bar a while longer, making small talk, and then decided to sit at one table for dinner.

"Are all of you guys thinking of going on the tour to the private beach on Wednesday?" Jimmy asked, looking around the table. They all nodded in the affirmative. "We keep saying how interesting he is, and how well he gets his points across, but I'm beginning to wonder about what he's really trying to get at. What do you think Earl? I believe he talked to you first, last night at the party."

"I just think he's a really nice guy who's interested in how people live, and not afraid to speak his mind. He never seems to condemn you, just asks how you feel about life and compares it to his feelings. What's interesting is that when he talks about something like racism, even though you never think you are racist, he gets you to really examine your feelings to see if maybe you might be. And then he has this ah, ah, theory whereby even if we are racist, it's somehow not our fault, because we were conditioned to feel this way by our parents or peer group when we were young."

"But then, he makes you feel that if you are, maybe you should take a hard look at what you believe, and change it if necessary," Marjean said. "Of course this is not the easiest thing to do, because in a way, this is who we are and how society works. You know I did social sciences in college, and we had classes, for example, one called Marriage and the Family, when we did take a hard look at some of these rules and think they were illogical, but then we're out of college, and have our own families and we often go back to the same rules. He definitely makes you think, but about simple, everyday life."

"His explanation about the politics of conservatism and liberalism was also quite simple, but very well stated. My minor in college was history, and I studied it with a great deal of interest, but never really realized that all those autocratic leaders had it worked out, and still do today. I always thought that public education was a relatively modern phenomenon, but it could have been taught over a thousand years ago. They knew the basics, and the clergy were educated. They could have taught the peasants too. They just wouldn't, because they couldn't control educated people as well as the ignorant."

"Well we didn't expect a vacation like this," Billy said, "but I must say we're having the greatest time with the combination of going to the beach, riding on the ferry, driving around St. John and visiting a real slave plantation and then having these great discussions. We'll probably need a vacation when we get back home."

They all laughed at this remark as they passed the wine around the table.

"And my husband even got some homework from Mr. Ricky. I hope he studies hard and gets a good grade," Katherine said.

"As you can imagine, I've been thinking a lot about that. Basically Mr. Ricky said to me, 'why are you an Independent and not a Democrat'. And after listening to him talk about the definition of the two, I really have to wonder why I'm not a Democrat, or a liberal, as he puts it."

"Never expected to hear you admit that," his wife said.

"Well, I'm still thinking about it, but as Mr. Ricky says, you have all these sayings about the political parties that are vague and really don't say much."

"You mean those sayings about freedom and government and regulation," Luke said with a smile.

"Yeah, you know what I mean."

After dinner the group went back to the bar for a last drink before retiring to their respective rooms. They asked Barry several questions about Mr. Ricky. His early life, his years in college, what he did before driving the taxi van? Was he always so interested in social values and politics? Did he work anywhere else? But they didn't get much from the stoic Barry. He kept grinning and telling them that Ricky would tell them everything they needed to know.

Chapter Eleven

Chapter 11

On Tuesday Ricky spent the morning at the Commissioner of Education's office. He was a consultant to the department, working with a team on including tourism as a part of everyone's economic existence on the island. There was a gap in this regard between the native St. Thomians and the residents from the Mainland, and Ricky was working hard to have more locals involved in the industry. He believed that the local involvement was going to come from the younger generation, and he was working with the school board to introduce more classes that included the economics and responsibilities of tourism. He had been getting a very favorable response, and the government was quite pleased with his work. Ricky had been the assistant Commissioner of Urban Development before deciding to become a consultant and taxi-driver, and was very aware and comfortable with how the local government worked.

Ricky then had lunch with his wife, Annette, and reminded her that they were going to Browning Beach the next day.

"It sounds like you're really enjoying this group," she said in between sips of iced tea. "You think they'll appreciate being introduced to our little organization?"

"Yes, I do. I can get them to think outside their comfort area, and they don't necessarily agree with me, but I think we have a good enough relationship that they're willing to listen to me and then give it some deep and intelligent thought. I was really pleased with how the trip to St. John went yesterday, Wally gave an excellent presentation and overall explanation of how Annaberg operated. I could tell they really gave the plantation and slavery a lot of thought, but they weren't completely overwhelmed by it, and were very willing to talk to me about other aspects of life in the V.I."

"So you think this couple you told about living here are really serious?"

"I could actually see them making it work, but I wanted them to get a good understanding of the pros and cons."

"And you're good at that, honey."

"Thank you, I try," he said and leaned over and kissed her on the cheek.

"So, going back to the group, you think they'll be totally surprised when you tell them about your ideas about the rules of society?"

"I'm sure they'll be a little surprised, but I believe they're already starting to figure out what I'm getting at in my conversations with them individually."

"Well hopefully they won't be so conservative that they think you're trying to introduce some kind of leftist philosophy to the world."

"There's always that possibility, unfortunately. But I don't think this group is that far right. But you know if they are, those are the ones I want to reach."

"By the way, that new reporter from the Daily News, Paul Newman, telephoned yesterday about talking to you. I think it's about how many recent high school graduates are going into the tourism industry. People seem to be very interested in your program right now. I didn't give him your mobile phone number as I didn't think it was that pressing."

"I met him a couple of weeks ago, and he said he was thinking about doing a story on the program. He probably has some follow-up questions. I actually floated the idea to him that we should develop a community college that has several courses, but specializes in tourism related jobs."

"Well, give him a call when you have some time. I think that community college idea is excellent; we can probably get more of the students in the nursing department as well, instead of having to import nurses from off island all the time."

"Yes, my dear, it would definitely be very productive to have more nurses trained on island. It shouldn't be that difficult once we get the program set up. I thought you would have been able to do it, but you had to do several courses in Puerto Rico to get your R.N. But it certainly gives us something to work towards."

"Speaking of nursing, I need to get back to the hospital. I have to take care of a few pressing issues so that I can take the day off tomorrow, but I should be at home by seven, so we can have dinner at home tonight at seven thirty. Philip said he'll be at home early as well. I'm thinking of doing my eggplant parmigiana."

"Sounds good," Ricky said getting up and kissing and hugging his wife. "See you tonight."

After lunch Ricky checked with the front desk at Sapphire Resort, and was told that eight guests would be going on his tour with him tomorrow. That meant Luke would be coming with one of his sons, probably the older one. He then checked out his van and did a little housekeeping to make sure it was clean and worthy of a tour event, before calling the Browning house above the beach, to confirm that he was bringing a group for a visit tomorrow.

Chapter Twelve

Chapter 12

The next morning when Ricky got to the kitchen for his customary cup of coffee, he noticed the newspaper in his chair, instead of in its usual position on the table. When he picked it up to put it next to his coffee cup, he realized it had been unfolded and then refolded. By the time he was ready to drink his coffee, both Annette and their youngest son, Philip, walked into the kitchen, smiling broadly.

"So have you read it yet?" Annette asked.

"You mean the newspaper?"

"Yes."

"Not yet, but I can see someone has."

"We both have. Look at the headline," Philip said.

Ricky slowly put down his cup, picked up the newspaper and carefully unfolded it. The headline read. "Top Three Candidates Prepare". He started reading the article and saw that it was about the reporter's opinion of the three leading candidates for governor in the upcoming election later that year. Paul Newman was the reporter who wrote the story, and he considered Ricky to be one of the three local favorites for governor of the U.S. Virgin Islands.

"Is this the guy who tried to reach me yesterday?"

"Yes, I believe it is. I take it you didn't have a chance to talk to him."

"No, unfortunately I didn't. If I knew the article was about this I would have spoken to him, but I don't think it would have made much difference. He was ready to spring this surprise on the residents of the V.I., no matter what I said. I just wish he didn't list all my academic degrees, as I think this might make it harder for me to get visitors to buy into our little organization to lift the ridiculous burden society places on us."

"I don't think this will make much difference, unless of course you do become governor and you just don't have the time."

"Don't be ridiculous. You know that's the farthest thing from my mind. I'm more than happy to do whatever I can to help any governor, but I have no desire to be one right now. Anyway, I just hope this group today doesn't see this article, I think they may all be ready to become part of our organization to end social conditioning."

"It will be fine, honey, whether they see it or not. These people seem to already be taken by you and your slightly un-conventional ideas."

"You mean our ideas, my love."

"Yes, Ricky, our ideas."

"Let me read this article in detail to make sure I don't have to sue the papers for libel or something," he said laughing out loud. "Then we have to get ready to leave. I promised the group at Sapphire to be there at eight thirty, so that we can leave around nine. Is your cousin going to pick you up for school, Phil?"

"Yes, Dad, he'll be here at eight."

Ricky turned into Sapphire Resort at eight fifteen, parked the van, checked in at the front desk to get his passenger list, then he and Annette walked into the breakfast area next to the main bar. He saw several members of his group at a double-table, went over to them to say good morning, introduced Annette to them, then went over to an empty table with her, where they had some toast and coffee in preparation for their trip.

Their server had just finished filling up their cups, when Marjean came over to join them.

"It is so good to meet you, I'm Marjean," she said to Annette. "Mr. Ricky has told me quite a lot about you, and even though my husband Earl and myself only met him a few days ago, we feel as though we've known him for a long time."

"It's nice to meet you too, Marjean. Ricky has told me about you guys too. And he does have that effect on people whereby he can make them feel completely at home with him in a short period of time. Even when they don't agree with him he does this. I wish I had this quality, especially in my job as a nurse."

"Yes, you're so right. He gets you to tell him all kinds of things about your life, and you don't even realize you're doing it. He just has this ability to ask these really simple questions about everyday life, and then they lead to more serious or complex subjects, and before you know it you're discussing areas like religion or racism."

"I know what you mean, Marjean. You can imagine what a struggle it is when you don't want to tell him something. Like if we're having a surprise party for him and he suspects, he will find a way to get it out of you. I often tell him he would have made a great lawyer if he didn't enjoy driving his taxi van so much. When he was in college here, he could easily have gotten into pre-law, but even then he had started to drive the taxi."

"Well, dear, someone had to make some money to pay the bills when we were both in college back then, and driving visitors around our island, was always a great way for me to do it. Besides being paid, I got a great education, not only from the many interesting people I met, but also really getting to know the island well."

"I don't know if Mr. Ricky told you, but Earl and I were in college at the same time too, back at the University of Tulsa, and we both had jobs and worked quite a bit when we were there. I really believe more students should do that. It's like a whole education in itself, just to learn how to balance classes and work schedules."

"Yes, you're so right, Marjean. This is all a part of college-age young people learning how to function in society. Time management is very important. It's probably something that should be formally taught. There's an area you can look into with your social science background."

"There you go again, Mr. Ricky, coming up with a really good idea out of nowhere. And I need to get back to breakfast. Just wanted to say hello to Annette. I'm sure we'll talk later. We'll all meet you in the main lobby at nine. I'll make sure everyone goes to the bathroom before we leave," she added with a laugh.

Twenty minutes later, Ricky got up, indicating to his server that he was ready to leave. She came over with his tab which he signed and returned to her, along with a five dollar tip.

"Why thank you governor," she said quietly, "appreciate that. Very nice article about you possibly being the next governor in today's paper."

"Thank you, young lady. I'm honored and humbled, but please keep it quiet for now. I don't think I'm ready to be governor yet."

"Oh, I don't know about that Mr. Ricky. I think a lot of people on the island believe you would do an excellent job."

"Thank you, thank you. And now I really do have to leave."

The group took their seats in the van, with Earl sitting next to Ricky in the front passenger seat, and Marjean sitting next to Annette, behind him. Jimmy was in the seat directly behind Ricky.

"Should be a perfect day for the beach," Ricky said. "We'll be going over to the north side of the island to a small beach that's fairly isolated and just in front of a local family's property. What makes it private is that you have to go through their property and therefore get permission to access the beach. Of course if you come in from the ocean that's not necessary, as every beach in the V.I. is public."

"Yes, I think we all know about that," Marjean said. "It's a great law for the residents."

"It wasn't easy to pass," Annette said, "but the government definitely did the right thing for the local people."

"When you have a visitor economy as we do, it's important for locals to feel that they are a part of the business of tourism and their way of life hasn't been taken away from them for the sake of profit. Especially if they perceive the profit is being made by people coming in from outside and don't care much about the island. It's quite a balancing act sometimes."

"So, this is something you work on too?" Earl asked him with a sheepish smile. Both Jimmy and Marjean chuckled when they heard this question.

"Well, if you remember, I think I mentioned that I do a little bit of consulting as well, on occasion. And basically I have a friend at the Department of Education who asks me for a little advice on how to prepare the older students for life after high school, especially as it might pertain to the tourist industry. It's really not much different than discussing with a fellow taxi driver what his son is going to do when he graduates, but it's obviously on a bigger scale."

"So, you're saying that you do more than just driving the taxi van and talking to your passengers?"

"Yes, I do a few other things from time to time. I mean, you know, sometimes it takes a little extra to pay the bills, especially with one son in college and another one probably going there soon."

"Yes, you have to pay those bills," Jimmy said trying hard not to laugh.

Annette turned to Marjean and shrugged her shoulders and opened her palms to ask what was going on.

Marjean smiled and pointed at Jimmy's backpack, where you could see the top of the newspapers. Annette caught on instantly, and also broke into a smile, but said nothing.

The group was fairly quiet on the way to the beach. They pointed to the automobiles driving on the left hand side of the road, and were enthralled by some of the steep climbs up the little mountains on the island and then the steep descents. It wasn't long before Ricky announced that they had arrived at the Browning Property. He called on his cell phone to say that he had arrived, then he drove past the house, close to the pink oleander bush that was just beginning to bloom. He drove around to the right of it on the dirt road that descended steadily to a makeshift parking lot, then brought the van to a halt.

"Here we are, folks. The Browning Private Beach." Ricky announced.

"Yes sir, your excellency," Jimmy said.

"Pardon me?" Ricky said, turning around.

"He said yes sir, your excellency," Earl repeated, and then started laughing. Several of the others started laughing too.

"Honey, they all read the article in today's newspapers," Annette said.

"Oh, they did, did they?"

"Yes, we sure did," Earl said. "What a great article. My God, it seems that the people in these islands want you to be their governor."

"That's just a little article about a new journalist's opinion. The other two guys are much more qualified."

"I don't know about that," Jimmy said. "that guy's a good writer. Sure did a lot of research. How come you didn't tell us you had a PhD from Stanford?"

"I don't like to make a big deal about that. You guys asked if I went to college and I said yes, the University of the Virgin Islands, which is where I got my B.A. but apologies if you thought I misled you. I didn't think my graduate degree had much to do with what we were talking about. Anyway, we're here, so let's go enjoy the beach. There are two small changing rooms down to your left as you walk down, and a toilet just behind them."

Ten minutes later they were all on the small beach in swimwear, lying or sitting on towels. There were two large mango trees behind the group, which gave some of them the option of lying in the shade. Ricky and Earl were the only two in the shade. Ricky having told him that he would get more than enough sun when he went into the water.

"I hope you don't mind me bringing Brandon along," Luke said to Ricky. "I was going to send him with his brother to go with this family I met to the tennis courts and then to the pool, but he asked me to come with me, and really seemed interested."

"No problem at all," Ricky said. "I think Brandon is quite mature, and very capable of understanding the stuff we talk about." Brandon grinned sheepishly, but nodded to indicate he did understand.

"So all the stuff in this article. Is it really true?" Jimmy asked.

"The factual information is true. I was fortunate enough to get a PhD in Sociology at Stanford, but a lot of the election intrigue and speculation is just that, speculation. In fact I was supposed to return a call to this reporter yesterday and forgot. If I had talked to him I would have made sure he didn't include me in this front page story. So please don't give it much credibility, I'm not going to be governor of the V.I. in November."

"But we knew you weren't just an average taxi driver taking visitors around your island, and this showed us why everyone we meet seems to know you," Billy said.

"That's true for a lot of people here. It really is. We're a very unique island. And some of my taxi driver friends are also very well known on the island."

"It's true," Annette agreed.

"So, Barry at the Sapphire Bar told us that you might have something to tell us," Marjean said, "and now that we know about your qualifications and positions in the local government, we're really intrigued."

"This week I've been very privileged to have some good conversations with all of you guys. And I've also been able to drive you around, especially in St. John with our tour to Annaberg, and discuss the terrible institution of slavery. And as bad as that was, it was in the past, and as a sociologist I'm more concerned with how we live our lives today. I've had conversations with you guys on many relevant social topics. Racism, religion, sexism, homophobia, politics, to name some of the main ones, and I've talked about how we're all socialized to think and believe a certain way about them from when we're quite young. Some of these rules are good, like being good students, being polite, learning self-discipline, being kind, but some of them are very negative and hateful and destructive to the idea of human kindness and love for one another. Unfortunately we are also taught or conditioned or some may say brainwashed, to believe that our religion is the best one, or our race is the best one, or our way of life is the best one, and unfortunately these ways of thinking have actually led to wars and a lot of useless killing in our world."

"So the next question is how do we change these negative rules into something more positive? If we don't recognize that we have them I don't believe we can change them, and we're condemned to continue with the same hurtful and negative thinking and behavior. Now, many of these social rules are completely illogical. To assume that one ethnic group is inherently better than another is nonsense. To assume that women can't do anything except wash and clean and raise children is nonsense. To assume that one illogical religion is superior to another is nonsense."

"So, I've formed a group, or organization if you will, called 'Life of Logic', and I ask people like you guys if you want to join. Basically, I ask you to examine your own lives, and if you agree with me, try to change the negative and illogical rules that you've been taught. And I ask those of you who are raising children to be mindful of the rules you're teaching them and try to make them logical. The third category is discussing this with people that you know or live with, family, friends or co-workers and see if they're willing to live according to more logical rules."

"I really believe if people started to do this, as simple as it appears, with enough numbers, we could change humanity for the better."

The group was silent for a while, obviously thinking about Ricky's little presentation. He casually held hands with Annette and waited for a response.

"I think we all felt that this was the sort of stuff you believed in from the conversations you've had with us, but I don't think any of us thought you had formalized it to the point of having an actual organization that presumably people join." Marjean spoke slowly.

"Well, don't think of this as any strict organization or club or anything like that. It's just that if you agree with me and try to get people to implement more logic in their lives and you succeed, I'd love to hear about it; or maybe if you get others to do the same, that would be even greater. And to be honest, this has to be done on a low key basis, and not by forcing people to think the way you do. And remember, a lot of these ideas have already been set in motion and are being utilized by millions of people, but there are still a significant number who want to keep it the way they learned."

"And they're probably all conservatives," Jimmy said with his big smile.

"Yes," Ricky said. "Most of them probably are."

"I think I'm beginning to understand."

"And guys, this is something you have to really believe yourselves. If you disagree with me, that's okay, then you don't need to talk about any of this to anyone. But if you agree with me, I believe we can make a difference. Just to get anyone who has been conditioned to live in a world of illogical ideas to think about an alternative is a positive step. Now I think we should take advantage of this beautiful bay, and go in for a swim, and we'll talk some more during lunch."

They all got up and went into the ocean, except Ricky, who stayed put under the mango tree so that he could keep an eye on everyone.

The group spent about an hour in the water. They laughed, splashed, swam, floated and talked about Ricky's proposition. He could tell when they were doing this, when they stood in a little circle waist deep in the water. Even the fourteen year old, Brandon, was nodding his head and talking in the group, to indicate that he was engaged in the conversation. Annette was swimming around more on her own, while the others were doing this.

They came out of the water, dried off and each had a drink from the two coolers that Ricky had brought. At noon, the group had some lunch, which Ricky had arranged for them. A small SUV pulled up with Ramos Restaurant written on the sides. A young couple got out, and served the group rice and red beans on paper plates.

As they ate, they spoke with Ricky.

"Mr. Ricky, I think we are all pretty much in agreement with your logic based philosophy for living," Jimmy said slowly.

"I'm so glad that you can see what I'm trying to get across to you. The rules that we're all conditioned with are very strong, especially since they usually come from people we love and trust very much, our parents. But unfortunately they're often handed to us the way they were handed to them, and it's not easy to say 'wait a minute Mom or Dad, that doesn't make any sense'. I saw you guys talking to Luke, and even Brandon, and I can tell you, teachers are probably the most aware of these illogical rules. This is especially apparent when P.E. teachers or coaches are around the same kids, say from age six to about twelve."

"I could see that quite clearly when I was substitute teaching elementary school," Katherine said. "They would go from these little angels who all loved each other, to being macho or feminine and sexist and even racist."

"And they got that way mostly because of what they were conditioned with as they were growing up." Ricky continued.

"So what do you think of all this?" Marjean asked Brandon, and then added, "hope you don't mind my asking him, Luke?"

"Not at all, he's mature enough to answer. And maybe it's kids his age that we need to get through to, but it's very difficult when they're still living at home."

"I definitely think what Mr. Ricky said earlier is completely true. I'm aware of it, because my Mom and Dad discuss it all the time. They don't only tell us how to act or behave, but how to deal with the kids who have become hateful, who want me to be like them. And I wish the kids all had parents like mine so they could talk about why we believe in certain things and not others, but most of them don't, and it's hard for them, as they have to learn to deal with how they're treated by themselves."

"Do you see much racism in your school?" Marjean asked.

"Yes, it's there, especially in the last year or two, especially when girls start to be interested in boys, and boys in girls. We had an incident recently where this kid who was White, liked this girl who was also White, and wanted to be friends with her, or go steady, but she was more interested in this Asian kid, and the White kid teased the Asian kid about his race, and then tried to fight him, but a teacher ended it. But you can see this kind of behavior going on below the surface a lot, although it goes away most of the time."

"We have a nephew about your age, and he says the same thing goes on in his school," Carol said. "So I guess racism is still around in our schools."

"It's gotten better," Luke said, "but unfortunately from a high school teacher's point of view it is still there. And when the political atmosphere is more sensitive like right before an election, the incidents of racism or sexism, become more prevalent. And when I see the negative behavior in the kids, I'm sure most of it originates with their parents, and this is why I'm in complete agreement with Mr. Ricky and his philosophy of living in a more logical manner, instead of upholding the nonsensical and made up rules that often depend on the justification of the nonsensical and made up rules of religions."

"Thank you, Luke," Ricky said. "It means a lot to me to hear you say that, and as I said, you're in the perfect position to see these travesties as they develop."

"You're right, Mr. Ricky. This really helps to clarify your points even more for us," Jimmy said.

"So how do we go about joining this alliance, or organization as you call it."

"I like that word, alliance. I guess that's what it is. I think I'll use it. Thanks."

"Sure, happy to help," Earl said, beaming.

"I'm going to have a little informal gathering at the bar at Sapphire on Friday night, and I was hoping we could all meet there and talk about Life of Logic with some other friends who have been practicing the concept in their lives, and out in the world. Most of them are from the island, but we have a few who are visitors. We also have some letters and cards and other communication from some of them telling us how they're doing where they live. It's not very formal, but it gives us a sense that some of our friends in the alliance, really believe it's important. Anyway, you guys can talk it over some more. We finished eating about a half hour ago, so you can go back in the water if you want to, or take a walk to the other side of the beach, or take a few photos, I saw some of you brought cameras, and it is a beautiful day."

"Is Mr. Ricky going to go in for a dip?" Earl asked.

"As a matter of fact, I will go in for a dip, as you put it." He motioned to Annette to stay behind while he went into the ocean, and together with Marjean, she walked to the chairs where they could keep an eye on the beach.

"I know you've probably shared the same opinion as Ricky regarding society's ridiculous rules for a long time," she said to Annette, "but did you think it was a little strange when he started asking visitors how they felt about the matter?"

"Actually no, it made good sense. We were actually frustrated for years, knowing how so many adults were able to negatively influence their children, and not be able to do much about it, but when the idea came to Ricky to put his ideas to visitors, it helped us feel as if we were doing something that could make a difference."

"What about that article placing Ricky as one of the top three candidates for the position of governor of the V.I.? That's got to make him one of the best known residents, and certainly one of the most important people. Was the article a surprise for you guys or is this something you talk about? And he's so nonchalant and laid back about the whole thing, like it's no big deal."

Annette smiled broadly and held her friend's hands in hers. "You know, you and Earl have gotten to know Ricky well in just a few days. It's amazing. He really is very laid back about this whole matter, but also very serious. The reporter called me yesterday and asked me to have Ricky call, but he said he thought it was about something else, and didn't. But I believe he knew it was going to be about the gubernatorial election, and didn't want to stop him. He doesn't want to be governor now, but he wanted to get his name in the conversation. It would not surprise me if he did become governor in the future. And I sincerely believe he would be very good at the job."

"But it must make you so proud to think that he's that close to being governor of the territory. The person in charge, having a great influence on people's lives. A guy with all kinds of academic qualifications and not only does he drive a taxi, not considered a great job by most, he's more than willing to have people believe that's all he does. He really doesn't seem to care what people think of him. That's amazing. That's a very powerful personal characteristic."

"As I said, honey, you guys do have a good understanding of Ricky. He really does talk about working hard and doing his best, and trying to live in such a way that it doesn't matter what others think of him. What probably concerns him the most about this whole governor business, is that he doesn't want anything to interfere with his Life of Logic project. This is what matters to him the most. He really feels that he's found his life's work."

"That is so good to hear. Not only is he a great guy with a great idea, we really believe that he's hit the social nail exactly and precisely on the head, and there's no doubt that if more and more people used logic to live by instead of all these ridiculous rules they would care more for their neighbors, and the world would be a better place to live in. He's so incredibly right."

Annette leaned her head backwards, looked up at the sky, and laughed in anticipation of what she was about to say to Marjean.

"This is an example of how Ricky sees the ridiculous in life, but it's how his mind works. A few years ago, his older sister was spending some time with us at his parents' home, and Ricky had been telling her that she was getting too old to wear those extremely high-heeled shoes, and he warned her that if she wasn't careful, she would hurt herself. His sister laughed at him and told Ricky that he didn't understand women and how important it was for their legs to look good. Of course Ricky told her in no uncertain terms how ridiculous it was that women would give in to some stupid rule about legs looking good that was obviously made up by men. Anyway, that night, his sister did actually have an accident when she was going down the stairs at her party, and badly sprained her ankle. It took several days for her ankle to improve and feel somewhat normal again, and even though Ricky chided her for not listening to him, he was really kind and took the time to help her ankle heal. So, he talked about women wearing high-heels a lot, and how ridiculous it was, and what a great example it was of something that was completely illogical that millions of women felt they had to do because of society. In fact, I believe he sees high-heels as a symbol of the illogical rules he talks about. Our son made a big joke about it when he suggested that Ricky should have a photo of high-heels on his van, with the caption, 'Think Logically'. Ricky thought it was pretty funny too."

They both laughed heartily at this.

"But you know," Marjean said, "he's so right. Wearing uncomfortable, dangerous high-heeled shoes, is one of the stupidest things a woman does to please men."

"Yeah, you're right. I never have. I've been lucky to have known Ricky so long."

"Ricky is certainly unique and special. I should say Mr. Ricky. I don't know why, but it sounds better to us to call him Mr. Ricky. Such a great character."

"That's funny, even the governor calls him Mr. Ricky."

"You mean the governor knows him?" Marjean asked.

"He's been one of the governor's chief advisors for several years."

"So in a way, he's already running the V.I."

"I never thought about it that way, but I guess you could say that."

Shortly after, Ricky walked past Annette and Marjean, waved at them, went into the van, and came out with two paddleball sets.

"Going to get some exercise," he shouted at the women on his way back to the beach.

While the group was playing paddleball, two men in Rastafarian dreadlocks hairstyles, walked up to them, and stood behind Ricky who was involved in a heated rally with Jimmy.

"Nice shot, Guv," the older of the two said. "Looks like you in good shape."

Ricky turned and scrutinized the speaker for a few moments. "My God, that's you, Joseph? So you finally decided to locks up. Looks good. So how are you and the rest of the Brothers doing on the farm? We had some good rain in December, so the crops should be good."

"Not doing as good as you, Mr Ricky, I mean Guv, but the boys are doing well. We had a pretty good tomato yield this year, and the cassava we've been experimenting with has been going good."

Joseph was a farmer on the north west side of St. Thomas, in an area known as Bordeaux. A number of young Virgin Islanders, most of whom were members of the Rastafarian Religion, had decided that they wanted to have an occupation whereby they provided fresh food for their fellow residents. This was in keeping with some of the philosophy of the Rastas, who believed in going back to and living off the land. Ricky who had known Joseph since he was a young boy, had been very helpful in getting the local government to find some land on the island that could be used for farming. This was not easy, as land is expensive and sometimes difficult to attain on a small island in the Caribbean, but Ricky was able to help the project work out for the farmers.

The group had stopped what they were doing and gathered around the three men as Ricky was talking to them. He turned and introduced the farmers to the group. The other one was Joseph's cousin, Donald.

"So you guys are farmers on St. Thomas," Jimmy said, "that's great. I grew up on a small farm in Upstate New York, and really enjoyed making things grow. I know originally there was some agriculture on the island, but didn't realize it was still going on. Us dumb tourists think that everything on St. Thomas is about tourism, but we're learning that there's more to it."

"Well, if you listen to Mr. Ricky, he will enlighten you. He has a strong grasp of just about everything that goes on in St. Thomas. He will make a great governor," Joseph added with a broad smile.

"Oh, stop that," Ricky said. "You know those crazy political articles trying to predict the next governor are always wrong. I wish they didn't write them, they give people the wrong impression. You can't be governor if you don't run for the office."

"Maybe we'll write you in. You'll have the most write-in votes in our history," Joseph said.

"I grew up on a farm too," Carol said, "until I was about twelve and my parents moved into the city. I remember how difficult it felt for me to move, as I really loved my life on the farm. Even though I was by myself a lot, I never felt alone. It was as though I could communicate with the land. It was simple, but I always somehow felt I was doing something important and meaningful. Not like city life which seemed full of silly made up rules. In fact, Billy and I are hoping to be able to afford a small farm sometime in the future; hopefully sooner rather than later."

"You certainly sound as though you and the farm communicated well. And you understood the beauty of resurrecting food from the earth. I wish you guys the best in getting your own place."

"Thank you," Billy said, "we're really looking forward to it."

"So, has your wife joined you on the farm?" Ricky asked. "I know she was afraid you guys couldn't make enough of an income when you first started."

"Once she saw that we could make enough to live comfortably from it, she jumped right in. I think she's even more consumed with farming than I am. It's like the plants become her pets, and she takes care of each one individually. Besides the planting, she also enjoys the fresh food we get to eat."

"What kind of animals do you guys raise?" Jimmy asked.

"We have two dogs and two cats, but we don't eat flesh," Joseph said, smiling at his joke.

"Is that because you're a Rastafarian?"

"All Rastas are vegetarian, but I was vegetarian long before I went Rasta, thanks to my good friend here, Mr. Ricky. He told me that eating meat was just something we were indoctrinated with when we were very young, and we just all accept it and never ask the question why. And we become so used to it that it becomes an addiction. But I'm sure Mr. Ricky has talked to you guys about all the crazy stuff we learn when we're young that doesn't make sense, but most of us never change. That's his main philosophy, and I must say I've always thought he was right, ever since I was quite young."

"Yes, Mr. Ricky has made quite an impression with all of us about these rules for living that we all learn as children. But was it difficult for you to stop eating meat? Was it hard to get healthy, tasty meals that didn't have meat? Did you miss the taste of it?" Jimmy spoke slowly as he asked these questions.

"I was in a position where either my wife or I put our meals together, so it wasn't difficult to find tasty food. I also did this because of how I felt about animals. Since I was a young boy I was very close to my pets, and when I understood the reality of how many animals are slaughtered for food, it was quite easy for me to stop eating them, and I can say for a fact, I never missed the taste of meat. And once I subscribed to Rastafari, it was never a consideration. What was also important, was that my wife had no problem becoming vegetarian either."

"So, have you been a farmer a long time?" Carol asked.

"When I was young most people who had room, grew vegetables or fruit on their property, and my family always did, so I learned how to make plants grow, and how to get food from them to eat, but there was never enough land to grow plants commercially until we got the Bordeaux grounds. And thanks to Mr. Ricky and his allies in our government, it has worked out very well."

"Have you lived here most of your life?" Carol continued.

"Except when I went to college at U.C.L.A."

"So you didn't go to the University of the Virgin Islands."

"I thought I was going to, but Mr. Ricky knew the track coach and he helped me get an athletic scholarship."

"So, you were on the track team?"

"Yes sir. I was a sprinter. Hundred to four hundred.

"And what did you study there?" Luke asked.

"I have a Master's degree in Agricultural Economics."

There was complete silence as the group stopped talking, looked at each other and smiled. Annette, who had come over, smiled too, then she spoke. "I know what you guys are thinking, here is a taxi driver taking visitors around St. Thomas and he has a doctorate, and you meet a Rastaman who farms the land, and he has a master's degree." They all nodded as she continued, "but this is not the norm on the island, at least not yet, but we're working on getting as many local kids as possible to attain a college education."

"That's great," Luke said, "absolutely wonderful. There's really nothing more powerful in people's lives than a good education. That's how we protect ourselves when people try to take advantage of us by telling us nonsense. I try to get my young students to understand that every day."

"That's how the wealthy stayed wealthy and the poor stayed poor for centuries," Ricky said. "The peasants had numbers, but not the education to know how to use it. Anyway, when my good friend, Joseph here, isn't working on the aeration system at his farm, he works on getting some of our Caribbean islands to improve their agriculture output so as to bring down the cost of living for the population and improve the income of the farmers. The cultivation of cassava on a large scale is probably his main concern. But let's go back under the tree and have some cold drinks. We can talk there."

They all walked back to the two mango trees, changed into dry clothes, got something to drink from the coolers, and made themselves comfortable, mostly sitting around in the picnic chairs. Joseph and Donald sat on either side of Ricky, each sipping from bottles of water.

"I've had bread made from cassava flour," Jimmy said. "It was quite tasty. I had a neighbor who was originally from Guyana, and apparently they eat it there. It was like a flat bread when I had it, but I guess they can make it as loaves too. This was several years ago, and even then, he was talking about how to get more people to eat it instead of traditional wheat bread. Is that true, Joseph?"

"Yes sir, you on the right track. This is especially true for the islands that were colonies and are now independent. As colonies they were used to eating the kind of food that their European owners ate, but a lot of it was imported. Of course the Europeans loved this, because the food was imported from them. And the governments of course imposed taxes on the imported products."

"So they were basically conditioned to eat European food," Jimmy said.

"Sounds like you've been speaking to Mr. Ricky." They all laughed at this. "Well, yes they were conditioned to eat it, and became addicted as well. So when the countries became independent, the governments wanted them to change to more local food, because that was better for the economy, and also cheaper for the population, but it was very difficult to get people to give up their addiction, and I believe some governments actually were voted out of office because they tried to get people to eat different food. It was like taking their alcohol away. But as time went on and the various populations became more independent and began to understand more about the importance of economics, they began to eat and be willing to cultivate more local foods. But they're all different. I was in St. Kitts which was a British colony, and they were all growing local foods and fruits for drinks, and very positive about it. Now, in Antigua, it was completely different and to them they thought the idea of eating cassava instead of flour was some kind of punishment. But a friend of mine from St. Kitts told me in some of the islands, residents were more British than the British."

"So Donald, are you in college yet?" Carol asked the younger Rasta.

"Not yet, Ma'am. I just graduated high school last year, and I took a year off from academics to learn about farming, but I intend to start at our local university in the fall semester."

"Do you enjoy farming?" Carol continued.

"Very much. In fact I'm hoping to work it out so that I can still spend a lot of time on the farm when I'm in college."

Joseph and Donald stayed with the group until their bottles of water were empty, then they got up and excused themselves, as they had to take produce from the farm to set up at their stalls in town for the weekend, where much of it was sold.

"Really nice guys," Marjean said as the Rastas walked away.

"You got that right," Jimmy said. "Makes us really think about moving here. Everyone we've met on the island seems so positive and upbeat. And Joseph talked so naturally about the problem with people being conditioned to do illogical things, in this case, to import food to eat, when they could grow what's native to the island. It really fits with what Mr. Ricky has been saying."

"You're right," Ricky commented. "Joseph gave us a very practical example of how being indoctrinated can cause people to have problems. So often it's just simple, mundane things."

"How should we expect this meeting to go on Friday, Life of Logic, as you call it? Must say, it has a nice ring to it." Jimmy sipped his light beer as he spoke.

"Well, I wouldn't call it a formal meeting," Ricky said. "We're just having a casual meal and talking some more about our idea on how to get people to change their ingrained but often illogical and hurtful rules they live by. Most of the other people there will be from the island, and they've all bought into our philosophy and will tell us if and how they've been able to influence people to think more logically."

"I think the two hardest areas to get people to see differently, will be racism and religion, especially the latter," Earl added. "Do you really think all religions are illogical?"

"Yes, I do. However, I do believe in the natural desire of people in a community to want to get together every so often to check on their neighbors and make sure everyone's doing okay. This is why I've been looking for an organization that welcomes everyone of every religion, and even those of no religion, to come together and provide a form of togetherness, in spite of the differences. And I believe the Unitarian Universalist Organization fits this bill."

"So we should try to get them to join?" Jimmy asked with a laugh.

"Not at all. It's just something similar to religion to talk about, if people insist on being a part of a religious-type organization. It shows the acceptance of different people who have different beliefs, without saying that one is better than the other, just because it happens to be the one your parents were indoctrinated with, and passed it down to you."

"This should be a very interesting get-together. I'm really looking forward to it," Earl said.

Chapter Thirteen

C hapter 13

Two days later, Ricky and Annette walked into the Sapphire Beach Bar and waved to the group who were all sitting at two tables joined together at the back of the bar area. They then paused and said hello to Barry who was behind the bar with two iced teas ready for the two of them. They took the drinks and said thank you to Barry with a slight bow, then they walked away and sat at separate tables. There wouldn't be any live music until later, but a Bob Marley song was playing, "Don't worry 'bout a thing."

Ricky sat at five different tables and spoke in an animated manner with all the inhabitants. He laughed, nodded to agree with them and constantly shook hands. These were people who liked and appreciated each other and really believed in trying to change the way society operated. Ricky went back to the bar before talking to the people at the other tables. He told Barry it was time to bring out the simple buffet that the Resort had prepared for the occasion, knowing that the drink prices would more than pay for it. Barry got on the phone, called the kitchen and watched as the three servers brought the dishes for the gathering. He next got on the microphone and announced that dinner would be a buffet.

"Looks like even less meat this time," he said to Ricky as he handed him another iced tea. "That's a lot of rice and peas and spaghetti, practically no fish."

"Yes, we're gradually getting the meat down."

"Did the matter of vegetarianism come up with the group this week?"

"Yes it did," Ricky said, "we met up with Rasta Joseph and his cousin at Browning Beach and talked a little about it, and also had some excellent rice and beans which I believe everyone enjoyed."

"That's such a big part of how ridiculous the rules of life can be. We're so conditioned to believe that we have to eat animals. And there's absolutely no logical reason for it. When we were in school on the island together, everything except for dessert was meat, meat, meat. And almost everything was imported. We didn't even know what meat we were really eating." Barry laughed cynically and shook his head.

"You're so right, brother. This was one of the first areas that got me thinking about all the nonsense we humans do, not only to our fellow humans, but to animals too. To raise animals as if they're tomatoes or broccoli or rice to be eaten is true cruelty."

"So Barry, you believe some of our illogical indoctrination has to do with what we eat too. I was thinking about that when

Marjean and I were talking about being vegetarian." Earl had stopped at the bar on his way back from the bathroom. "When you think about how animals are treated before they're slaughtered, it is cruelty, but what we eat is such an addiction, that it must be pretty hard to get people to change their habits."

"It is, but my good friend, Mr. Ricky, here, got me to see the light. I must say, when he first told me about being a vegetarian when he came back from Stanford, I thought he was nuts. But I can definitely attest it wasn't that big of a deal to give up eating meat, and it made me feel a lot better about myself."

"That's great," Earl said as he walked back to his table.

"You're a good man, Barry, with an excellent understanding of life," Ricky said.

"I have a great teacher."

"I learned a lot from you, Barry, long before I ever went to college. Don't ever forget that."

"Thank you for the kind words. Yeah, I guess we did go through a lot of life learning and questioning back then. Now you need to go and hob knob some more with our friends, especially the newer ones, then give us all some good information from the stage."

"Yes, you're right," Ricky said, "don't want it to get too late." He patted Barry on the shoulder then moved away to the buffet, where he helped himself to a salad and some spaghetti in marinara sauce and headed for the nearest table.

He moved around the room to each table, and saved the one with the current group, where Annette was now sitting, for the last. He was soon there.

"Hope you guys got something good to eat, and are enjoying the evening."

"Yeah, we certainly are," Jimmy said. "Young Brandon has been filling us in on some more of the attitudes of kids his age. Very interesting."

"It's been very interesting for me too," Luke said. "Parents don't get to hear all of this stuff at home."

"So what behavior from your classmates bothers you the most?" Ricky asked.

"I would say Racism is the worst. I just think it's terrible to treat someone badly, or speak about them as though they're worthless or even a bad person, just because they happen to be a different race from you. And it's not out loud or obvious, but some of them, and it's mostly guys, remind you of this in some way, every day."

"That's a good observation, Brandon, thanks. Do you think if their parents taught them we're all the same when they're younger they would be different?"

"Yes, Mr. Ricky."

"And that folks, is exactly the kind of racist attitudes we're hoping to change."

Ricky stayed at the table for about fifteen more minutes and spent most of it talking to Jimmy and Katherine about the logistics of moving to St. Thomas. At about eight-thirty, he excused himself, got up, pushed his chair back, and walked over to the stage where the bands played. A young man and woman in their mid-twenties, pulled up a table and three chairs to the stage, along with two large briefcases. They quickly took some manila folders out and laid them in order on the table. Once they were finished, Ricky walked up to the microphone stand, took out the mike, and addressed the gathering. He didn't want to give a big speech that seemed as though he was convincing these people to join his organization, he wanted them to view this as something they had already agreed with, and if it didn't cause a major problem, they could ask people they knew to think about it, and think about it themselves, especially if they happened to be raising children. He said a few words about the group he had the pleasure to personally meet that week, and indicated where they were sitting. Ricky said he viewed a Life of Logic as something completely normal, which everyone should be using, simply because it caused a lot less conflict among people and made the most sense.

The one organizational action that he asked was they keep in touch with him in St. Thomas and they ask people they talk with to do the same, so that he could have some idea of how people were reacting to the Life of Logic concept. So he made sure all the new people had contact information for him and his volunteer associates. He also asked the couple at the table to let them know how many people had contacted them since the last meeting six months ago.

The young woman strode up to the microphone, greeted the gathering, introduced herself as Adriana and announced that the folders contained notes they had received from eight thousand, three hundred and eighty people who claimed this was an important and much needed endeavor. She read a few of the notes: "Thanks for the enlightenment," one said, "We walked away from religion and are much happier," another said, "We understand the stupid rules much better," another said, and several other similar sentiments. She then invited the audience to look through some of the notes when they were finished talking. There was an orderly, but very noticeable round of applause when she sat down again.

Ricky took the microphone, thanked her for her work and commitment, told everyone that they would also have a general hand out for them at the bar, to remind them of the illogical rules that they were hoping to change - racism, sexism, homophobia, eating meat, and religion being the main ones. He then announced that the band would start playing in fifteen minutes, and brought his little presentation to an end. He felt it was very important not to turn this into a long drawn out affair. After he put away the microphone and helped spread out the folders, he returned to the table with Annette and the group.

"Very good talk, Mr. Ricky," Earl said. "Not too long, to the point and very positive. As you said, you don't want people to feel like they're joining some kind of big organization. By the way, Marjean and I are returning to Oklahoma tomorrow, and we'd be most grateful if you could take us to the airport."

"Certainly; what time is your flight?"

"It's at eleven a.m."

"Okay, I'll be here to pick you guys up at eight thirty. Maybe next time you can stay longer; really get to know the island."

"Yes, that's definitely our plan."

"I thought I should let you know that I met a couple from New York today, maybe ten years or so older than me, and I got into a pretty good conversation with them regarding your philosophy." Jimmy said. "They said they thought what I said made sense, and even added to it, with things like clothing and the way we dress. They thought it's not easy to get people to make changes about their habits, but if enough people agreed, they could see how we would all get along better."

"That's great," Ricky said, "good work. It feels good when people agree with us."

"I tried it with a guy I met too," Luke said. "He seemed very interested at first, but then he told me he used to be a pastor, and tried to convert me to Evangelical Christianity. But I'm going to meet with him again. Who knows?"

They all laughed when Luke said this, as did he.

"Oh, you're definitely going to get some of that, you just have to keep trying if they'll keep talking to you. This is good to hear that you guys are already talking to people about the importance of logic in life," Ricky continued. "Before you know it, it will become natural to you, and you won't even have to think about it consciously."

A half hour later, Ricky and Annette had one dance together, and then decided it was time to head home for the night. Ricky reminded Earl about the pick up time in the morning, stopped at the bar to say good night to Barry, and then walked out to the parking lot.

Chapter Fourteen

C hapter 14

The next morning, Ricky and Annette arrived at the Sapphire Resort, to take Earl and Marjean to the airport. The couple from Oklahoma was waiting for them in the main lobby. They had already checked out, and were sitting in a corner next to their suitcases.

"Good morning," Ricky said as he walked over to them. "You guys are looking well. I take it you didn't spend all night at the bar and got some sleep."

"Good morning, Mr. Ricky and Annette, we had a few dances, then headed to bed. I must say I was beginning to get that calypso rhythm when Marjean pulled me away. I even had a couple of dances with that young lady I had to apologize to. She's a good teacher."

"Good morning folks," Marjean said. "Yes, Earl was definitely dancing to calypso music, but unfortunately the music and his body weren't quite connected. He has the moves," she said, starting to laugh, "but now we have to work on his rhythm. She even had him doing the limbo. That was scary. I had visions of having to call an ambulance for him."

"Sounds like you guys had a very interesting time," Ricky said. "You know Barry is going to tell me all about it. I hope someone took some video. We could use it on our national ads, showing a visitor enjoying himself."

"And then the band played some Bob Marley music, and the next thing I know is that he's now dancing reggae." By now, Marjean is bending over with laughter. "And he is better at reggae than calypso. At first I didn't think he knew there was a difference, but he did catch on, probably because there's less movement. And then he started telling everyone who would listen that he knew everything about reggae music, because he met some Rastas at the beach and they explained it all to him. Then he started on about the deeper meaning of Bob Marley's song 'Don't worry 'bout a t'ing'. How it meant that everything in life would be good if we all went back to living off the land and not eating meat and taking care of nature."

"Sounds like he had a few rums before bedtime," Ricky said.

"Actually he didn't have much to drink, just had a good time dancing to the music."

"It was great. Just when I get the hang of it we have to leave. I've got to find a Caribbean Club to go to somewhere in Tulsa."

Just then the rest of the group walked into the lobby to say goodbye.

"Good morning, guys. Glad to see you got up in time to pack," Jimmy said with a big smile. "That was quite the performance on the dance floor last night. I can't believe Marjean had the time to teach you all those moves, especially the reggae part. Those images will be with me for a long time."

"Well if you decide to move here you'll have to work on your dancing to fit in. Several people at the bar thought I was a local resident," Earl said in between chuckles.

They were all laughing when Ricky announced that it was time for Earl and Marjean to leave for the airport. When Ricky picked up a suitcase and headed for the door, Jimmy pulled Earl to the side.

"Make sure you keep in touch, my friend," he said, "and let us know how it goes when you tell Mr. Ricky what you told us last night. That should be very, very interesting."

"I'll be sure to let you know," Earl said, and the two men shook hands.

"There's an envelope here for you," the Front Desk Manager said to Ricky in a loud voice. "It was dropped off yesterday."

"Thank you, Miss Eileen," Ricky said. He walked back to the counter, opened the envelope and took some cash out of it."

"Is that from the hikers in St. John?" Jimmy asked.

"It sure is my friend," Ricky said, putting the envelope in his pants pocket.

"You were right, Mr. Ricky. You were right. Must be nice to have that kind of faith in people."

On the way to the van, Ricky said to Earl and Marjean, "You guys check and make sure that you have your ticket and I.D. and anything else that you need to travel?"

"Got it all here, Mr. Ricky," Earl said.

Just before the van turned left out of the resort's main entrance, Marjean tapped Earl on the shoulder to remind him that he had something to say to Ricky, who pulled off the entry way so as not to impede traffic.

"Okay, what did you guys forget?" Ricky asked.

"We didn't forget anything, but we have a confession to make," Earl said. "Our flight doesn't leave until one o'clock, and we need to have some time to talk to you about something fairly important. I mentioned it to Annette and she said you didn't have any other appointments later this morning, and we could all go to a restaurant. We apologize for misleading you about the time, but we're sure you'll find this very interesting."

"And you knew about this, Annette?"

"They told me a little bit last night, and I think it will be a nice surprise, but you need some time to sit down and listen to it."

"Now I'm really interested," Ricky said as he turned out the main gate.

"We hope you guys enjoyed your week," Annette said, "and you got a good feel for what the island is like."

"It was great," Marjean replied. "Wish you'd been able to spend more time with us, but I know how busy you are at the hospital. Maybe next time; and yes, we're already thinking about a next time. By then Earl should be a great dancer to calypso music. I'll see that he gets some practice. I bought a few CDs." They all laughed at this. "And the group that you put together, Mr. Ricky, was excellent. We got along well, we were really intrigued by your discussions about the ridiculous rules of life, and the visit to the sugar plantation was great, as well as meeting the Rasta gentlemen. And on top of all of that, we had a wonderful time at the various beaches, just enjoying the water and soaking up the sun, maybe except for Earl here who soaked up too much of it and almost had to spend his vacation indoors."

"Sorry Dear," Earl said facetiously, "I'll be better next time."

"So, you guys go back to work on Monday, or do you have a few more days off? You probably need some rest to recover from your vacation," Ricky said.

"Marjean has until Wednesday, but I go back on Monday," Earl said.

"I guess that oil company really needs you," Ricky added.

The ladies giggled when he said this.

"Well, that's kind of what we want to talk to you about."

"What, you're resigning? You want me to find you a job here in St. Thomas? You'd have to live in St. Croix, that's where the oil refinery is. You know this is getting quite suspenseful. Now I can't wait to hear what you have to say."

They all laughed at this, and ten minutes later Ricky pulled into Vinnie's Italian Restaurant, which served breakfast and was quite close to the airport.

"Remember, you can always find vegetarian food at an Italian restaurant," Ricky said as they walked through the front door of the restaurant.

"Good morning, Mr. Ricky, or should I say Governor Ricky," a young man with fairly short dread locks said, as he put four menus on the table.

"Good morning, Young Dread, and please ease up with the Governor stuff. You guys want to eat, or just coffee for now?"

They agreed on coffee and waited until the server poured and then moved away before the mysterious conversation began.

"So, go." Ricky said to Earl with a smile.

"First we want to apologize for not telling you the truth, but Marjean and I aren't who we said we are. By that I mean we are married and live in Tulsa with three kids, as we said, but I don't work for an oil company, I work for the University of Tulsa, we both do. And we're basically here to check you out, and the way you explain and promote your illogical, life rules philosophy."

"Hmm, go on."

"I'm the vice chairman of the Department of Social Rules and Behavior at T.U. and I was asked by a committee formed by the chairman, including the university president, to look into your philosophy and see how we can study it and use it in our curriculum."

"Our president is also good friends with the president of Stanford, and he had him check with some of your professors and also your dissertation. Apparently you've been working on this for a while."

"Since my teens, but how did you guys learn of it?"

"From a new professor who visited St. Thomas a couple of years ago, and went on some of your trips. He was really impressed by your whole presentation, as we are. And when this article came out about your being a top candidate for governor, that gave you even more credibility. In fact I spoke with my chairman about it yesterday. Apparently what they all want you to do is start out by writing a book. They will take care of all the publishing and distribution and of course, your fee, which for an academic book will be quite sizable. Except I don't think it should be very academic, just a simple story about a family who changed their illogical rules of life and made everything work much better. Or it could be a group of people like us, who fix our own families through our Life of Logic, and tell others how to go about doing it. I really believe this could start an incredible revolution in the improvement of life worldwide."

"I've talked to several professors in the history department at T.U. and they all think it's a great idea," Marjean added.

"I suppose I'll have to take some trips to present my ideas. Do you think I could drive a taxi around Tulsa while I'm there?" he said with a laugh.

"Oh, stop with the jokes," Annette said. "This is really good news. Probably what you've always wanted."

"Yes, it is good. Very good. If we can get people to examine just the basic socialization: their illogical religion, their illogical racism, their illogical sexism, I really believe that it could make a positive difference on a large scale, and college is probably the best place to begin the process, simply because people involved in higher education are more used to using logic than those who aren't. But ultimately we have to get Life of Logic out to everyone. If the rules we live by improve the quality of life, then we will have a better world."

"You are right, Mr. Ricky," Earl said.

"What do you think should be the book's title?" Ricky asked.

Annette spoke slowly, softly, but clearly. "Mr. Ricky's Life of Logic."